Blueprint

Theresia Enzensberger

TRANSLATED BY LUCY JONES

dialogue
books

DIALOGUE BOOKS

First published in Germany in 2017 as *Blaupause* by Carl Hanser Verlag
First published in Great Britain in 2019 by Dialogue Books

10 9 8 7 6 5 4 3 2 1

Copyright © Carl Hanser Verlag GmbH & Co, KG, München 2017

Translation © Lucy Jones 2019
Preface © Lois Innes 2019

The moral right of the author has been asserted.

Photo: Bauhaus-Archiv Berlin (original photo in black and white,
re-colouring by Carl Elkins for Studio Mierswa Kluska)
Lyrics from 'The Lavender Song', English translation © Jeremy Lawrence

A CIP catalogue record for this book is available from the British Library.

Hardback ISBN 978-0-349-70081-6
Trade Paperback ISBN 978-0-349-70082-3

Typeset in Berling by M Rules
Printed and bound in Great Britain by Clays Ltd, Elcograf S.p.A.

Papers used by Dialogue Books are from well-managed forests
and other responsible sources.

Dialogue Books
An imprint of
Little, Brown Book Group
Carmelite House
50 Victoria Embankment
London EC4Y 0DZ

An Hachette UK Company
www.hachette.co.uk

www.littlebrown.co.uk

Theresia Enzensberger studied Film and Film Studies at Bard College in New York and writes as a freelance journalist for the *FAZ, FAS, ZEIT Online, Krautreporter* and *Monopol*. In 2014, she founded the award-winning BLOCK Magazine. *Blueprint* is her first novel. Theresia Enzensberger lives in Berlin.

Preface

The Bauhaus led a brief, yet seminal life. Founded in Weimar by the pioneering modernist architect Walter Gropius, the German arts and crafts school was operational between 1919 to 1933, and is considered to be the most revolutionary artistic movement of the 20th century. With utopian visions for the future, the school was notable for its rejection of classical teaching methods, and radically sought to merge artistic practice with the emancipating advancements in industrial production.

It enrolled both male and female students alike, appointing Wassily Kandinsky, Josef Albers, Gunta Stölzl, Laszlo Moholy-Nagy and Paul Klee amongst its most influential tutors. Despite varying in artistic approach, they came together in the pursuit of an all-encompassing art form, one which was no longer preclusive of interpretation, lofty or unattainable – but to be found in the fabric of everyday object.

After its three successive locations in Weimar, Dessau and Berlin, the school was eventually closed by the Nazi Party in 1933, who had denounced it a hotbed for fanatical, communist ideology. But they were much too late – the Bauhaus tradition had already reached the shores of the US, where many of its members had fled before the Second World War. Since then, the movement has become synonymous with both modernist design and theory, and stands as an enduring testament to the phenomenon of this short-lived school.

The central character in *Blueprint* is Luise Schilling, a young female student who is beginning her first day at the Bauhaus in Weimar in 1921. She is from an affluent Berlin family who, despite being sceptical of her enthusiasm to study architecture, afford her the luxury of her own privately rented room. Luise's privilege does not extend to any sense of self-importance, however, which is apparent in her relaxed, affectionate relationship with best friend and fellow student, Maria.

At the onset of the novel, Luise is presenting her portfolio to the school's director, Walter Gropius, who is depicted as a distant, imposing figure – yet one she is nevertheless enamoured by. When he finally admits her to the course, she meets his rather impassive gesture with a brimming sense of pride. Here begins Luise's most disquieting tendency, which is apparent throughout the novel: her holding-up of all self-worth in the eyes of men.

She becomes infatuated with the elusive Jakob, and quickly immerses herself amongst his cult of friends; Samuel, Sidonie and Erich. Distinguishable by their strict vegetarian diets and crimson monkish robes, the 'cowl-wearers' adhere to the spiritual doctrines of Mazdaznan; a mystical, pseudo-religion advocated by the Bauhaus' preliminary course leader, Johannes Itten. This new-age movement was ostensibly concerned with the total purification of body and mind, and at first, Luise is subsumed into fairly innocuous rituals – meditation and spiritual excursions among them.

But as she grapples with the increasingly mercurial affections of her new friendship group, she engages in practices that become much more sinister – masochistic, even. In doing so, she unwittingly stumbles upon a truth most young women must reconcile with in their pursuit of acceptance: that is, to be desired is to necessarily punish oneself. After rejecting the ideology and rituals of the Mazdaznan community, Luise gradually distances herself. The supposedly enlightened group appear to her to be equally as unwavering as her Fascist-becoming brother, and on the order of her family, she leaves Jakob and Weimar for good.

The novel's first section, contained in Weimar, and its second, in Dessau, both reflect the political and cultural shifts in the schools' movement across Germany. These geographical locations and their spirits also serve to offset Luise; put simply, she is forever an outsider. When Luise returns to the Bauhaus in Dessau, determined to enter the newly formed architecture course, it's now a well-oiled, municipally funded school, enabled at a time of rising economic fortune. But following her brother's refusal for financial support, she must now tirelessly work to pay her own way. Her vulnerability is further highlighted with the introduction of her new, frenetically disposed partner, Hermann – his liquor-filled soirées feel both exhilarating and uneasy, as if he is yielding her towards his recklessness. The ambiguities that envelop their hedonistic relationship become clear when their passionate relationship reaches its peak.

Mercifully, Luise battles on, developing her own plans for a modern housing estate which she determines to present directly to Gropius. Despite her repeated relegation to the female domains of the weaving workshop, and the stubbornly persistent sexism she continues to endure within Dessau's newly formed architecture course, Luise finds a personal resolve that is commendably unshakeable. For all its proclamations of equality and liberalism, the Bauhaus proves decidedly resigned in any attempt to subvert bipolar concepts in gender capability. Luise must find her own way under the glass ceiling that is all too familiar.

As a young female architect myself, I sat down to read *Blueprint* expecting to be more familiar with the contextual references. But, despite being separated by a century, Luise's story felt similar – in fact, uncannily like my own.

In 2014, I was a twenty-year-old, image-conscious undergraduate who was just about to commence her second year of architecture studies at the University of Brighton. In common with Luise, I'd spent my first year living wildly, moving frenetically from one friendship group to the next, and with my newfound independence, I was caught up in a whirlwind of hedonistic distraction. But our long summer break had afforded me some downtime, and I reflected on what had been a distinctly uninspiring introduction to a course I'd waited so long to study. For everything that was going on around me – from the excitingly anarchic sounds of electronic music my new boyfriend had introduced me to, to the social-media-inspired watershed in mainstream feminism – my course felt comparatively stale, slow to react and decidedly male-oriented. To my lecturers, Le Corbusier seemed to be Modernism's only poster child, and the rigid set squares and drawing boards we were tasked to use felt like inadequate, outdated tools in which to represent myself and the world I was experiencing. Fortunately, I had the wholehearted support of my family, and was certainly never subject to any physical abuse. But those particular feelings of erasure, inadequacy or generally having to make it by oneself ring very true to me – even to this day.

Indeed, *Blueprint*'s author, Theresia Enzensberger, has chosen to position this novel at an interesting time. 2019 will mark a century since the founding of the Bauhaus, and in this way, the novel is in part a celebration of its life and influence. Through the experiences of a student, Enzensberger is able to animate this world in such a way that gives substance to the Bauhaus legacy beyond simply the icons with which we are familiar. But it is also those same icons we are encouraged to reconsider. We've certainly arrived at the mass production utopia the Bauhaus had hoped to achieve, but in all its ubiquity and homogenous effect, have we also lost the ability to find beauty in everyday objects? The disposable tendencies of IKEA would certainly suggest so.

Perhaps the most lasting effect of *Blueprint* is linked, both then and now, to the disturbing emergence of far-right thought – and ultimately what this means to a new generation of young women. The likes of the Me Too and Stop Trump movements are encouraging demonstrations of feminist advocacy and suggest that we are much quicker to articulate or call out misogyny than would have been the case a hundred years ago. But in the pages of *Blueprint* – in our desperation for Luise to see sense – Enzensberger likewise encourages an introspection, also reminding us not to overlook those certain institutions we deem safe or exempt from prejudiced thought. In this way, *Blueprint* could not be more well timed.

Lois Innes
June 2019

Weimar, 1921

I still don't know where the director's room is. According to the big clock in the foyer it's almost five, and I stray through the corridors, hoping to spot a sign somewhere. The hallways are empty. I can only hear muffled voices and noises coming from the depths of the building. The other students are probably still in their workshops. When I climb the long spiral staircase for the second time to reach the third floor, I see a group at the end of the corridor. But unfortunately, it's only Sidonie and the other cowl-wearers, and I don't want to look like the new girl in front of them on any account. So I walk past them, looking as purposeful as possible – they don't even seem to notice me – and then turn a random corner. I have to stop myself from cheering when I finally see the name *Walter Gropius* on a sign at the end of the hall.

In response to a surly 'Come in', I enter a bright room. There is a huge desk in the middle, buried under stacks of papers. Holding the telephone in one hand, Gropius stands at the window with his back to me. The thick cable coils to the base. He's taller than I thought, and even though I can't see his expression, I sense that he's used to being treated with the greatest respect. The conversation seems to go on for ever. Should I leave again? Pretend I never received the envelope with his invitation?

'Well, then please call me when you find out ... Yes ... and a good day to you too!' Gropius' manner is controlled, but his voice is thick with pent-up anger. He slams down the receiver on its spindly brass arms, then turns around and looks at me, his mind elsewhere. 'These bureaucrats!'

I nod, trying to show my solidarity with him against the ominous bureaucrats although he's not talking to me, of course.

For a moment, Gropius seems confused at my being in his room; then he collects himself. 'Come in, sit down. What can I do for you?' Now it's my turn to be confused. He's the one who asked me to come, after all, so why do I have to explain myself?

Perhaps institutional mechanisms at the Bauhaus work in the usual bureaucratic way – an invisible hand consisting of protocol, regulations and appointments bringing people together who aren't exactly sure how they ended up there. I explain that I'm new to the Bauhaus and that I was asked to introduce myself and bring my portfolio. Gropius' face brightens.

'Ah, that's right, a new student. Forgive me for not being able to see you earlier. I usually look at portfolios straight away so that you can start taking classes, but the past weeks have been very busy. Let's have a look,' he says, reaching for the large box that I have been clutching tightly all this time. During the next few unbearably long minutes that he spends immersed in my work, I look out of the large windows that face the summery courtyard.

I steal several furtive glances at his face, his high forehead and bushy eyebrows furrowed in concentration. Perhaps it's because of the call he just made, but his expression bears a gravity that emphasises his authority.

'It's unusual for students to join us mid-semester,' he says at last, returning my portfolio. 'How did you hear about the Bauhaus?'

He does not even mention the architectural drawings that I did at the office of a family friend, in the evenings after everyone had left. At the time I had felt so grown up, like a real architect surrounded by sharpened pencils, giant rulers and oily, translucent draughtsman's paper.

I explain that my father makes cast-iron purlins, which brings him into regular contact with the more modern architectural offices in Berlin, including Peter Behrens'. They are closely following the developments in Weimar. But if my father hadn't left a pamphlet lying in our living room, I would probably never have heard of the Bauhaus. He's always been sceptical about my enthusiasm for architecture and would be damned rather than tell me about a university where you can learn something other than good housekeeping. So I sent off my application in secret. When the acceptance letter arrived, it took some persuasion and my mother's complicity for my father to allow me to go. In the end, he gave his reluctant consent, probably because there is a weaving workshop at the Bauhaus.

Although I'd love an ally, I don't mention any of this to Gropius. For now, I let him believe that my family is fully behind my plan to study architecture. He stands up and says, 'Your drawings have potential, but we are very keen to offer our students a comprehensive education. In the preliminary course and other workshops, you will learn many things that will certainly help you with your architectural studies. If you have any questions, feel free to contact me.' I'm sure that these are the standard platitudes he trots out to every new student, but the idea of Gropius being my mentor fills me with pride.

~

Maria sits on my narrow bed, stuffing herself with the biscuits that Frau Werner has brought up to my room. The tea, which my landlady has brewed from herbs picked in her garden, smells suspicious. Neither of us touches it, but the sweet wafers are a pleasant change to the mush of vegetables served in the canteen. Maria rolls her eyes in delight, dangles her long legs over the bed and says while chewing, 'I can't believe that those silly cowl-wearers have got their way at mealtimes! I couldn't swallow a single mouthful at lunch today. God bless old Frau Werner and her fanatical baking!' Maria likes talking like this: full of ironic pathos and lots of exclamation marks. She feels at home here; very much at home, I think, looking at the crumbs on my bed.

I can't blame her for preferring my room to her cramped attic, but sometimes, it feels like she has moved in altogether. Her tall thin build belies her love of food and her inclination for drama. She has a gaunt face and large, moist eyes.

Although we both pretend not to care about Johannes Itten's cronies, we always circle back to them in our conversations. Most of the time we make fun of them – their brown, hooded robes that resemble monk's gowns, their strange customs, gymnastics and diets, and how sometimes, with no warning, they strike up a song in the corridor. I tell Maria about my meeting with Gropius and my wretched hunt for the director's room, which makes her laugh at me fondly. Then she returns to the subject we were on before. 'Seriously, though, they have some nerve! Ten people deciding what the entire college eats!'

'I hate the grub too. But I heard that the budget has been cut. Perhaps the school can't afford to buy meat any more?'

Maria shakes her head. 'I'm sure Itten's lot are behind it. I heard that they don't even pay school fees!'

'What makes you think that?'

'Some people say it's because they're Jews, and get favourable treatment.'

I haven't thought about the fees since I persuaded my father to let me study here. And I wonder how you can tell that somebody is Jewish, anyway. My brother Otto is constantly going on about the Jews. I only know one Jewish family, who live two houses down the street from our flat in Berlin. And only the father is recognisably Jewish because of his locks and skullcap.

Maria says, 'If you ask me, it's nonsense. Not all Itten's disciples are Jews. Most of them were already at his art school in Vienna and he probably made a deal with Gropius. Still, it's not fair.'

'That might be the case, but aren't we focusing on them too much? Maybe we should just ignore them,' I say.

'Ignore them! Easier said than done, those stupid songbirds

stand and chirp on every corner. If they weren't so cliquey, I wouldn't mind. But they won't even talk to us. And Sidonie is the worst. Who does she think she is?'

I happen to think that Sidonie is very beautiful, the way a few of her short red curls are always peeking out from under her hood. But I keep that to myself.

~

During the breathing exercises that we do at the beginning of the preliminary course, I feel the sweat running slowly down my spine. Usually I love the heat, more than your average European. I like it when even the breeze is so hot that it feels as though it's coming from an oven. I like it when the heat doesn't let up, even at night, and you have to throw off the bedsheets. But the large, curved windows of the workroom can only be cracked open, and the heat hanging over Weimar for days now is unbearable, even for me. On the positive side, I have been allowed to take part in lessons although I don't officially start until next semester. Sidonie and the others are sitting in the front row. They inhale and exhale so diligently, while everyone else just seems to be going through the motions. Johannes Itten is standing at the front giving instructions in a stern voice. We're supposed to take a deep breath and then exhale noisily through our wide-open mouths. I seem to be the only one who is trying not to laugh. But I'm also the only one doing this for the first time. Now Itten tells us to choose a scrap of metal from the pile lying on the floor.

'The goal is to understand the material. You can exam-ine materials in many different ways. Today, we're going to examine them from the perspective of drawing,' says Itten. He's wearing a floor-length purple robe that looks much more expensive and elegant than the coarse jackets of his acolytes. He does look a little bit like a monk, perhaps because his face doesn't reveal any emotion. His instructions sound like sharp commands, reminding me of my father. I stare at my blank sheet of paper and the crooked piece of metal lying on my desk like a grotesque, misshapen worm. I don't think Itten expects us to simply draw our piece of metal. I glance around surreptitiously. The others have all started. Unfortunately, I can't see how they're going about the exercise. Architectural drawings are different: there are no uncertainties. They have a clear aim, a design and fixed units of measurement.

I think back to my lonely nights in the studio. I had to beg my parents' friend for the keys, but at least I could work there in peace. Officially, I was with my friend Charlotte, whose parents are always travelling. Last year, I kept more secrets from my father and mother than ever before. Today I'm wearing my new carpenter's trousers for the first time. I went to quite some lengths to buy them, even hiding them under my bed. My father would have a heart attack if he could see me now, which is a satisfying thought. But in this heat, the trousers aren't the best choice; they feel tight, and my bottom is sticking to the wooden seat.

Up until now, Itten was sitting on his desk meditating with his eyes closed, his long thin legs entwined in a complicated cross-legged position. Now he is standing up to take a look at the drawings. I haven't even started. I hastily sketch a few lines on the paper to form a simple illustration of the piece of metal. I can't come up with anything better. Itten leans over my shoulder and looks at my sketch. He gives off an odour of garlic, beeswax and sorrel. Beads of sweat have formed on his bald crown. If I weren't so intimidated by his presence, I'd feel disgusted. A bead of sweat rolls so slowly off his shiny head that I imagine I can still prevent it from falling on my paper. The soft, thick drawing paper is absorbent, and small waves form around the puddle in the middle. The pencil line unravels in rivulets. 'You'd better throw that away,' says Itten; not because he has dripped sweat on to my drawing, but because I haven't accomplished the task. I look at him helplessly.

'Hold the material in your hand. Yes, like that. And now close your eyes. How does it feel? Try to internalise that feeling so much that you can draw it.' Then, he moves on to look at the next piece of work.

I still find the whole thing strange, but I try to participate in the exercise. After all, I don't want to fail. The metal is smooth and not cold like I imagined, but then again, nothing has been cold in this room for a long time. It also feels quite bulky. OK then, I think. I pick up my pencil and begin to do some shading. I don't get very far. The others have long since finished. Itten holds up a few successful drawings, gets the students to describe what is special about them, and gives us the next assignment: we are to go and look for interesting materials in the park on the Ilm. 'We'll meet again in an hour.' Everyone is relieved. No one could have endured this stifling oven for much longer.

~

Another assignment I don't understand. How am I supposed to know what Itten considers interesting material? I pick up a couple of sticks and branches, weigh them in my hand and toss them away again. I try to stay in the shade. The path is lined with large, gnarled trees. I've lost sight of nearly all the other students, but I'm quite happy about that. I'm too uninspired to be good company, and my trousers are still clinging to my legs. Further on, a tower appears between two trees – Gothic Revival, I think straight away. My knowledge of architectural history is patchy, but we had a magnificent book about Gothic architecture at home, which I flicked through from time to time. This building doesn't seem very old, meaning it can only be Revivalism. Why anyone would build in the same style aeons later is a mystery to me. And in Berlin it's got out of hand since the middle of the last century. They just copy styles from various eras and cobble them together. It's not very original. But maybe it's a sign of our times. No one wants to adopt an independent position or take something seriously.

I try to focus on the assignment instead of letting myself drift off. Perhaps there's something that could pass as interesting material near the Gothic Revival building. Next to the tower is a squat annex house. The walls are overgrown with ivy and a few trees surround it; an ornate balustrade runs around the flat roof. Its high stone walls, which are such a surprise to see here, give off a pleasant coolness, and a smell of mildew comes from the shaded parts. Atop of the sturdy columns that frame a large wooden door, two figures stand, tilting slightly forward. I stop and wonder who they might be.

'May I introduce you? Vroni and Peter, the Guardians of
the House of the Templars,' I hear someone say in a bright,
slightly husky voice with an Austrian accent. A young man
is sitting on the ground against the wall near the entrance,
looking up at me in amusement. He's about my age, and
his thick, blond curls and long lashes make him look like a
pretty, boyish girl. I must seem confused because he adds,
'That's what we call them. I haven't got a clue who they're
supposed to be. Saints, I suppose.' He jumps to his feet and
holds out his hand to me. 'I'm Jakob.'

Only now do I see that he's wearing a monk's jacket.
Strange, I think, I've never seen him with Sidonie and
the others.

I pull myself together. 'I'm Luise. And what are you
doing here?'

'Collecting interesting materials – what else would I be
doing?' he says and smiles in a way that is obviously meant
to be roguish, but which I can't seem to resist all the same.
I'm surprised I didn't notice him in class before.

He picks up two stones from the ground. One looks as
if it was carved as part of a relief and the other looks as if
it has been buffed smooth by water. I admit that I wasn't
sure before what qualified as interesting material – and
that while, sure, it makes sense that the contrast between
handcrafted stones and those shaped by nature might be
interesting, I still don't know what I'm supposed to look for.
Jakob grins again in the same mischievous way and offers me
one of his stones. 'We'll say that we went looking together.
Johannes doesn't mind us collaborating.' It seems strange
that Jakob wants to work with me, of all people, because the

cowl-wearers normally stick to their own, but I'm so happy that I agree straight away.

When we enter the workshop, most people are back, and some are already at work on their sketches. Perhaps I'm imagining things, but I sense that we're being scrutinised. Sidonie, most of all, gives us a probing look for just a little too long before turning back to her drawing. Jakob walks purposefully over to a corner away from the others, I follow him. When I confess that I haven't fully understood how we are supposed to feel the materials, Jakob gives me a lesson in what he calls 'material studies'. We both feel the stones with our eyes closed. A few times, I accidentally-on-purpose touch his hand, which doesn't seem to bother him. His earnest explanations are laced with pathos, but all the same, something about them makes me respect him. At least I think I understand the exercise now. We prepare drawings that are supposed to depict our perspectives of the two stones. I make a rubbing across some sand that I've scattered under the paper to give my picture the rough texture of the hand-sculpted stone. Then I apply pencil shading to the other drawing, so thickly that it shines like a pebble worn smooth by water. Jakob fills one sheet with small boxes, the other with wave-like overlapping shapes. His abstract draw-ings are very skilled. At the end of the class, our drawings are the ones Itten holds in the air.

~

Maria pushes the brown lentil mush around her plate with a spoon, perhaps in the hope of finding a piece of meat somewhere. She's so preoccupied with her food that I'm free to keep an eye out for Jakob. Strangely, I haven't seen him since the day he shared his stone with me. That was two weeks ago. How can a normal student not show up for lessons? I haven't seen him in Kandinsky and Klee's lectures on form and colour either. Maybe he's been expelled? That's only happened once in the history of the Bauhaus, so I've heard, to a student who didn't show enough commitment. But surely that would be news? Besides, he was taking his studies very seriously. What if something happened to him? Maria would have told me; she's always up-to-date on college gossip. Then again, I haven't told her about my meeting with Jakob, so she has no way of knowing I'd be interested.

We're sitting in front of the Prellerhaus studio in the shade of a low-hanging tree. This nondescript building is available to a few select students as living accommodation. A couple of men who excel in their subjects are allowed to work and live here in one of the spacious studio rooms. Women are not allowed to apply 'for moral reasons'. The canteen is located right outside, on the big square, in a house that used to be the studio of Alexander Brendel, a former director here. It has stone walls and a roof that used to look like a glass dome. But barely a single window has survived the war, and the roof is now boarded up with thick planks.

It looks forlorn compared to the main building, which reminds me of the pictures of the grand new buildings in Vienna. Leaves are already lying on the ground; the heat of the late summer has hardly let up in Weimar since August. We've put our plates on the wooden bench next to us. The other students are scattered across the square, some sitting on the floor, others on chairs that they have taken outside to use as tables. On the other side of the square, the cowl-wearers have sat down as a group. Jakob is the only one missing.

'Lu, why are you making that face all the time? It can't be this disgusting food because you haven't even tried it,' Maria says, giving me a nudge.

Before I can reply, a stocky girl and a long-haired boy come over to us. The girl starts chatting to Maria and very soon, the two of them are trying to outdo each other in sparkling conversation. The boy listens, either because he's too shy or because he doesn't want to vie for a turn to speak. His long hair somehow looks strange to me, and I try my best not to stare too much. The girl is talking about the kite festival. No one talks about anything else these days. There hasn't been an official announcement, but everyone is already speculating about possible venues for the after-party, the prizes and, most of all, their inventive kite designs.

'Hopefully, we won't have to go on strike again,' says the girl. 'It hardly makes a difference to workshop production on the pittance we earn, but we can't stop working on our kites!'

Maria laughs and is about to answer, but the long-haired boy suddenly pipes up and says, 'No one *had* to go on strike in spring, silly! It was a show of solidarity with the workers' uprising. People died! It's not something to joke about.'

The girl rolls her eyes and turns to me while her long-haired companion goes back to sitting in silence.

'It's bound to be less disorganised this time. It was our first festival last year and it started when a few people decided to fly kites as a bit of fun,' the girl tells me. 'After that, a crowd gradually gathered to watch, and by the time it was dark, the whole Bauhaus was out there. A few students played instruments, some danced, it got late, and at some point, Maria and I were sitting drunk on the top of the hill, watching the sunrise.'

'Stop!' cries Maria. 'You're making me all nostalgic. We're not that old!' She laughs her raspy Maria laugh.

This year, people say, the festival will be promoted officially with invitations designed by the Bauhaus workshops. A few students have agreed to play music for the dance and are already rehearsing. Afterwards, there will be a party organised by the teachers. The long-haired boy thinks it's likely to be at the Ilmschlösschen, but Maria claims that those rumours are nonsense; after all, the great outdoors was good enough for everyone last year.

I'm a bit envious of their memories of last year's party, but next year, I think, we'll all be reminiscing together. The whole Bauhaus came together last year, the girl said. The thought of seeing Jakob at the festival makes me feel elated.

~

In my room, there's only a little mirror over the wash bowl. I've hardly paid any attention to it up till now, but today I want to put on some make-up. I want to indulge the ritual, which makes you feel beautiful for a moment, steeled for a special evening. So I dig out the small silk purse filled with all kinds of cosmetics that Charlotte gave me as a going-away present, saying, 'So you don't fall apart.' All of a sudden, I miss her. We spent hours before big parties doing ourselves up in her parents' spacious flat on Kurfürstendamm. If she didn't like the dress I'd put on, which was usually the case, she looked me up and down with a critical eye, shook her head and flung at least four gorgeous dresses at me. She turned on the gramophone; we quaffed her father's champagne – he was never home – and I listened, riveted, as she told me about her latest conquests. I always admired Charlotte for her indifference to convention when it came to matters of love. If she took interest in a man, she started to view him as prey. Once she captured him, she would immediately cut him loose, and he would join her entourage of hangdog ex-lovers. I never enjoyed the kind of freedom she did in her parents' absence, but even if I had, I probably would have been too shy to take advantage of it. My conquests amounted to a stolen kiss from a family friend of my parents whom I had been in love with for years. And then there was the night with that awkward, pushy boy, which I had decided didn't count.

I look in the tarnished mirror and try to paint my lips neatly with dark-red lipstick. My thick brown hair has never succumbed to my attempts to tame it; I need an entire box of clips and hairpins to keep it under control. If Charlotte could see me now, she'd probably drag me back to Berlin on the spot. She had predicted that I would come to see my decision to study at the Bauhaus as a mistake. And she wouldn't be happy with the threadbare room that my parents rent for me from Frau Werner either. I also thought it was uncomfortable in the beginning, before I realised what an enormous privilege it is to have your own room here. Maria sublets a place on the outskirts of town. She shares her tiny room with a mean girl she avoids. In comparison, my room is downright luxurious, even though I sometimes miss my parents' house, with its high ceilings, paintings and dark-gloss parquet floors. But here I live near the park and have a desk, a chest of drawers and a fairly comfortable bed, which I've smartened up with a cashmere throw that my mother gave me. Frau Werner is a bit dotty but nice. She's the widow of a civil servant and sometimes has enough money left from her pension to buy real coffee or the ingredients for an apple cake.

I just hope that she doesn't knock on my door as I bend forward, attempting to draw a neat line across my eyelids. I step back to admire my work. I'm fairly presentable in my petrol-blue skirt and simple black blouse, which makes my eyes seem brighter – and anyway, the main attraction today is my kite, which I've spent every spare minute making. My four-headed hydra now lies crumpled on my bed. When the wind fills the papier mâché heads, I'm hoping they will spread out in all directions.

~

I spot Maria from far away. She's caught up in the strings of a red monstrosity that must be her kite. Her ambitions have surpassed her craftsmanship, but she isn't letting it ruin her good mood. She stands, laughing, among the folds of material, crowing, 'Maybe I should have sewn myself a ball gown instead!'

Students are scattered over the whole hill, busy with their kites. Everyone is running around and checking the craftsmanship of the others' creations. Some are squinting up at the sky with desperate expressions or testing the air with wetted fingers because it's yet another hot, cloudless day without any wind. I'm happy when the first few people start running in an attempt to get their kites off the ground. I want to show off my hydra, too. People certainly look impressed when its heads drift up into the air for a moment. But it's no use: kites don't fly without wind.

People sit down and chat instead. The first bottles of wine are opened and passed around, and I look for Jakob, a little less discreetly than before. He's nowhere to be seen. I'm surprised at the force of my disappointment.

I half-heartedly listen to the conversation that Maria is having with a boy from my preliminary course. She is extolling the virtues of the loom. She's been working in the weaving workshop for half a year and is very interested in the possibilities of the equipment.

'If you can mass-produce textiles, then you have to do it!'

Maria has found an appreciative audience in him.

'I think so too. Doesn't make them any less beautiful,' he says.

'I don't understand why some people are so against it. What's wrong with making an affordable carpet?' Maria is getting very worked up.

'It's absurd. They're snobs,' says the boy.

Just as I feel my way into the conversation enough to play devil's advocate, the musicians march past to our left: five men, emitting sounds from their trumpets and violins that amount to noise rather than music. A small man with unkempt hair walks in front of them, an enormous cardboard triangle on his head, shouting to those standing around, 'Follow the music! The music knows what's good

for you!' Students hastily follow his command and a procession forms behind the band. Our little group splits up
too: Maria links arms with the boy and they disappear into
the crowd.

After a short way on foot, we arrive at a detached brick
guesthouse with a garden. A sign above the ground-floor
windows says *Ilmschlösschen*. Everyone jostles their way
inside. The musicians set up on the stage. The hall inside
has been cleared of furniture and there is a bar at the other
end. Despite the strange march music that the band played
on the way in, it seems that they can also perform dance
music. At the parties I went to in Berlin with Charlotte, they
danced the Charleston, which seemed wild and provocative
to me. But here, dancing doesn't seem to follow any rules
whatsoever and no one cares about steps or a fixed partner.
As exciting as it is, it overwhelms me. I find the little pockets
of freedom that open up in restricted situations are often
more compelling than what happens in a complete vacuum.
But perhaps this isn't a useful principle; and all it does is
show my lack of creativity.

Suddenly, Jakob is standing in front of me. I look down at
the floor, which I'm somehow still managing to stand on. He
takes my hand and pulls me away from the crowd towards
the bar. 'Wine?' he asks.

'Don't you want to say hello first?' I ask back, beaming at
him all the same. His sudden look of unsettlement disarms
me because it seems out of place in his charm offensive. The
instant feeling of intimacy he creates seems authentic, at
least for him. I'm just about to ask what he's been doing for
the past few weeks when Sidonie turns up. She has two men

in tow, and they're wearing monk's jackets with starched collars, of course.

'Don't you want to introduce us, Jakob?'

I beat him to it. 'I'm Luise. Nice to meet you.'

'And you, Luise.'

It annoys me that Sidonie doesn't bother to introduce herself. I'm surprised to hear that she has an Austrian accent. Then I remember that Maria told me that Itten's crew were mostly from Vienna.

'And who are you?' I ask eventually.

'How silly of me, sorry. I'm Sidonie, and this is Erich and Samuel.'

Erich raises a hand, Samuel gives me a curious look. I don't let on that I already know who they are. Erich is a short man with a good-natured air, black hair and olive skin. He's a little older than the others and has a slight limp. He was probably on the front, I realise, which makes me sad. Then I find myself ridiculous. After all, I have no idea what it's like to fight in a war. It already seems so long ago. When the war ended, I was just a naïve teenager with little more on my mind than my next French lesson.

I would prefer to be on my own with Jakob, but the others don't show any signs of leaving. My sudden suspicion that there might be something going on between Jakob and Sidonie is hard to confirm or deny at first sight. But to be honest, it's only based on the cheap romance novels that I read in secret. And their plots would certainly feature the charming Jakob and wild Sidonie as a couple.

The band stops playing. Gropius walks on to the stage with a measured tread; silence immediately falls. I wonder if he's only just arrived. I haven't seen any of our masters yet tonight.

'Dear Bauhaus students! Tonight is a very special evening. I am delighted to celebrate this festival together with you, and I hope that there will be many more to follow.' Everyone has already drunk a lot of wine, and Gropius is interrupted by frenzied applause and heckling. He smiles and waits until the noise subsides.

'The lack of wind won't deter us. Prizes have been promised for the best kites – and prizes there will be.' More tumultuous applause.

'May I ask you to bring your kites to the stage? The judges will be Masters Itten, Klee and my humble self. We will retreat and announce the winners in half an hour. Until then, please do credit to our reputation and enjoy yourselves!'

I now spot Klee, whom my fellow students refer to as 'the Good Lord', perhaps owing to his rare sightings. Even now, his large, melancholy eyes drift across the crowd with a detached expression. He is standing to the far right of the stage next to Itten, whose hands are crossed in his robe sleeves, and whose expression is watchful and piercing. His outfit looks even more monkish in contrast to the tweed suits all around him. The Good Lord and a Buddhist, I think, and can't help grinning. The musicians have struck up a lively tune, which is possibly meant to mock the commotion that has broken out in the room. People jostle in front of the stage. In my distraction I've lost my Hydra. I must have put it down somewhere?

'You're not seriously going to take part in this circus, are you?' Sidonie asks me, with a sneer. I glance uncertainly at Jakob, who gives me a similarly pitying look. All of a sudden, the whole spectacle seems like a joke. Before I know what I'm saying, I've renounced my kite, along with the weeks I spent making it. The mood lightens.

'Excellent, then we can leave,' says Jakob. Leave? Where to? Is there another party that I don't know about? Sidonie, Erich and Samuel have almost reached the door. Jakob takes my hand and pulls me along.

~

The park is bigger than I realised. The others stride resolutely ahead. I don't know where we're going – my question gets lost in the conversation. So I follow, trotting alongside the others without saying anything. I work out from the conversation that they're all interested in a writer called Hanish, whose book has recently been published in translation. His 'magnum opus', as Sidonie calls it, seems to play a great role in their lives. I admire their earnest way of discussing literature and art. They sound much more intelligent than Charlotte's friends, whose clever witticisms and funny banter always seemed cynical.

In the dark, I need a moment to grasp that we're heading towards the House of the Templars, the building where I met Jakob for the first time. He finally turns to me and says, 'Do you remember those two?' and points to the statues over the entrance.

'Of course, Vroni and Peter,' I say. 'Are they your patron saints?'

Whenever Sidonie thinks I'm not looking, she gives me

one of her puzzled looks. When I look straight at her now, she smiles and says, 'Maybe they protect us, yes. But we don't have any saints.' She pushes open the wooden door. Are we allowed to go in? Is the building empty? Jakob takes a candle from a box and lights it. He shines our way down a gloomy corridor. We enter a musty-smelling room where colourful blankets and rugs are scattered everywhere.

In the far corner, there are easels, half-finished canvases and a low table where tubes of paint have been carefully arranged. There's an old stove built into the wall. The others move around the place, seeming so at home that I relax a little. Erich lights more candles and limps around the room to spread them out, Samuel looks for wine, and Jakob and Sidonie sit down with me on the blankets. 'Welcome to the House of the Templars,' says Jakob. 'Johannes is allowed to use the room as a studio. He lets us use it at night.' It takes me a moment to realise that he means Johannes Itten, and I'm impressed that he's on such friendly terms with our teacher.

Samuel comes back, triumphantly holding a bottle in the air. There is something unintentionally comical about him: his narrow glasses are a bit wonky, his brown monk's trousers are a bit too big for his skinny frame, and his hair looks as if he cuts it himself. There are no glasses, so we pass the bottle around the circle. Jakob and I make little figures out of the damp wine label which I find silly, but still engage in with great enthusiasm because Jakob is handsome and I'm tipsy. Suddenly, Sidonie stands up and says, 'If you insist on poisoning yourselves, then that's up to you. But I don't want to sit by and watch any more. I'm going out for some fresh air.' Then she leaves the room with exaggerated slowness to show that she doesn't need to slam any doors.

Jakob shakes his head. 'According to the Mazdaznan doctrine, we're supposed to renounce alcohol and tobacco,' he explains. 'Sidonie is a stickler for the rules. But she'll calm down.' *Mazdaznan*, whatever that means. I decide to finally ask Jakob a few of the questions on my mind. 'You don't know about Mazdaznan? Well, how could you, after all?' He seems happy about this. 'Johannes taught us everything. Mazdaznan is about living as much in harmony with yourself as possible and, ideally, about overcoming your ego. That's the only way to make art. We meditate and do gymnastics. But you know what? Just read about it yourself.' Jakob scrambles to his feet and comes back with a dog-eared book. On the blue spine in gold lettering, it says, *Mazdaznan Health and Breath Culture*, and below, the name I picked up earlier: *Dr O. Z. Hanish*. 'Take your time, but please bring it back. It's the only copy we have.'

Erich and Samuel have stood up. In his slow way of talking, which always makes him sound a little ponderous, Erich says, 'We're just going to see what's up with Sidonie. Are you coming?' To my regret, Jakob agrees, so we all go back out into the mild night. It is strangely bright: the moon throws shadows across the park grounds. We find Sidonie near the Sternbrücke, the bridge over the River Ilm. She has found a comfortable spot on the other side of the river and is dangling her legs in the water. Her mood seems to have improved.

'Come on, let's go for a swim,' says Samuel, who is already stripping down to his underwear, hopping clumsily on one leg while crossing the bridge. 'Great idea,' says Sidonie, pushing him. He manages to grab her hands and the pair of them land, shrieking, in the water. Having also stripped, Jakob asks, 'Are you coming?' and then dives into the river. I hesitate for a moment, trying to remember what underwear I have on. Then I overcome my shyness, remove my skirt and blouse, and follow the others. The current is so strong that I catch my breath, and the chilliness of the water wakes me up. Sidonie and Samuel have already drifted quite a way downstream. Jakob holds on to a tree root until I have caught up with him. The stones on the riverbed are slippery; I lose my balance and shriek. Jakob grabs me and, arm in arm, we set ourselves adrift on the water. His sudden, wet kiss takes me by surprise for a moment, but then I feel triumphant that I didn't just imagine he was attracted to me, and this mingles with my excitement into a heady euphoria.

Erich smiles indulgently at us when we return, dripping and freezing. 'Young people and their escapades,' he teases. I'm impressed by how he doesn't seem at all bitter about his handicap. Sidonie and Samuel sit down next to him, shivering. Jakob quickly pulls his trousers over his wet legs, then wraps his monk's robes around me and dries me off. The material is coarse and scratches my skin, but right now nothing can take away from the warmth spreading through me.

Back in the House of the Templars, it's as if nothing has happened between Jakob and me. Perhaps the atmosphere here is just too public or not special enough, but he doesn't pay me any more attention than the others. Samuel hands us all blankets and, after much fumbling, lights a fire in the hearth. We crouch in front of it, not speaking, and warm ourselves. The coal in the hearth is still glowing as we fall asleep on the rugs.

In the middle of the night, I wake to the sound of a drawn-out, terrified scream. It takes me a while to understand where I am. It's Erich. Frightened, I shake Jakob who is lying slightly apart from me. 'What's up?' he asks drowsily. The screaming has stopped. 'Erich was screaming, it was horrible. What's the matter with him? Is he in pain?' I ask in a whisper.

'Oh, it's just the nightmares he's been having since the war,' Jakob says.

'But should I wake him up?'

'No, there's no need. Just go back to sleep,' he says and closes his eyes. He falls asleep again straight away.

I lie awake and listen to Erich's whimpers, which start up again from time to time, turn into sobbing and eventually stop.

~

Given that I was the one who was set on leaving, I am surprised by the homesickness I sometimes feel during those first weeks. In the mornings, I walk to the kiosk, buy a newspaper and spread it out on the table. It's comforting because it's one of my parents' rituals. I picture my father poring over the rustling paper, a cup of black coffee next to him. I feel like an adult or like I'm playing adult, which in the end probably amounts to the same thing.

The little kiosk on Seifengasse also sells coffee, and on this particular morning, the sun is shining for the first time since the weather turned chilly and autumnal. Three out-of-work men are sitting on stools in front of the shop, and one of them makes a lewd remark as I walk past. Despite this, I still want a coffee before lessons start. Luckily, when I sit down, the men have become too engrossed in their conversation to pay me any more attention. I flick through the newspaper, but their discussion is so lively that I can't concentrate.

'That damned Brandenstein thinks that he can just ban any meeting if he feels like it!'

'That pompous Minister of State never thought much of the German National People's Party.'

'He won't let decent German workers meet in Weimar – but the communists can do whatever they like.'

'To prevent "riots". What a flimsy excuse!'

'It was obvious that they'd use the Erzberger case for their own purposes.'

'That weakling! He deserved it. If they hadn't assassinated him, he'd have sent Germany to the dogs with his politics. He was up to no good!'

'This whole government is dangerous. The Social Democrats want peace at any price, even if those agitators bring down the German nation for good!'

I leave half my cup of coffee, fold my newspaper and walk away. My brother Otto is always saying that the German Nationalist Party is good for getting rid of the communists. I'm happy that their meetings have been banned. I find their boozy events with all the jeering and howling deeply unpleasant. And the logic of these men seems pretty backward to me. Even I can see that Erzberger's murder was the result of right-wing agitation, so how can they turn the tables and accuse the others of agitation? I'm still too early for class, so I drop in on Maria at the weaving workshop.

She listens to my thoughts and says, 'You know what, Lu? You have to understand that people are really suffering in these awful economic conditions. The demands of the entente aren't easy to meet. The war was bad enough, so it's easy to see why people are worried about what's going to happen now. You're not affected, but you still see the way we live here.'

I'm about to contradict her and say that anyone can achieve whatever they want by working hard; but then I feel like a hypocrite. Unlike Maria and most of the other students, my parents support me financially and I've never had to worry about having a roof over my head or food on the table.

After class, I stand with Sidonie and the others in the courtyard and try to collect my earlier thoughts. Samuel is about to reply when Sidonie says, 'Oh, Luise, let's not talk about politics, it's so boring.' Instead, she talks about Itten's current work. It's a painting of his one-year-old son against a golden background. It is symbolic of the 'New Man', or the transparent race. I am starting to find her enthusiasm infectious. I only see Itten in class, but if what the others say is true, his genius finds little expression there. I keep trying to catch Jakob's eye. Although he pays me a little more attention than the others, nothing has happened between us since the night of the kite festival.

~

The rain lashing across the train windows transforms the passing landscape into motley greys and greens. Abstraction rather than impressionism – Jakob would appreciate it. Maybe he would make a few sketches for one of his paintings. He has missed the train, probably because he overslept or was 'distracted', as he likes to say. A leaden feeling of disappointment has become my second nature, I hardly notice it any more. Our night in the House of the Templars was two whole months ago. I've been tiptoeing around him ever since, as the heat of the summer has turned into the cold of November and the preliminary course has become my daily routine. One thing I've learned about Jakob is that you can be certain he rarely does what he says he's going to do. Sidonie and Samuel are asleep, she with her curly head of hair leaning against his shoulder. Erich is taking a later train. I can't help but hope that Jakob will join him and turn up in Berlin after all.

Charlotte told me in her last letter that she was 'over the moon' to finally meet 'the famous Jakob'. Just thinking about it makes me furious at him. How can I explain to Charlotte that Jakob only turns up when he seems to have nothing better to do? But that he never tires of saying that he likes me in a way he hasn't liked anyone in a long time? None of this makes sense, and even I only believe him if I try very hard.

At least I don't have to worry about how to introduce him to my father any more. On the other hand, it's very hard to say how Charlotte will react to my new friends. Either she'll find them exotic or she'll turn up her nose at them.

Samuel's glasses have slipped down his nose again. His

brown trousers are so askew beneath his monk's robe that they stretch tightly across his bony knees. I wonder whether they will take off their robes when we arrive at Anhalter Bahnhof. I would be embarrassed to tell them that their outfits are not appropriate attire for meeting my parents.

Maria disapproves of how much time I'm spending at the House of the Templars. Despite my attempts to explain what I like about these people, she still doesn't understand. She turned down my offer to come to Berlin with a roll of the eyes.

'We should have brought a present for your parents!' Sidonie exclaims. I can't help but laugh. Sidonie likes to play the unpredictable wild child, but she still hasn't managed to shake off her impeccable upbringing.

'My parents don't expect anything,' I say reassuringly. 'My father is mostly in his office, and my mother doesn't care about that kind of thing.' I try to describe my mother's warmth, but end up saying, 'You'll meet her very soon anyway. She's promised to pick us up.' Samuel is awake now and teases Sidonie for being so proper. 'So, the countess has remembered her manners, has she?'

'Shut up,' Sidonie says, laughing, and thumps Samuel in the side.

But Samuel is attentive enough to say in the end: 'Come on, Sidonie, let's change out of our jackets. We wouldn't want to seem weirder to Luise's mother than we already are.'

The conductor passes through the carriage, announcing: 'In a few minutes, we will arrive in Berlin's Anhalter Bahnhof.'

I feel nervous. We all agree that Weimar is a backwater.

Berlin is notorious even in opulent Vienna, but I can't tell what my new friends will make of my home town.

~

Our flat smells familiar: of floor wax and *Après L'Ondée*, my mother's perfume. The rooms suddenly seem enormous to me. The flowers set everywhere in vases by our housekeeper seem wasteful, the art on the walls old-fashioned. Samuel looks around shyly, unlike Sidonie, who behaves as if she has lived here all her life.

'I've made up the bed for you girls in your room, Luise. Samuel, you are sleeping in the guestroom with Erich,' my mother says.

'In the small guest room?' I ask.

'Otto is staying, and he has reserved the big one for himself.' I hadn't banked on my brother being there. He's been travelling for two years. He's supposed to take over Father's firm one day, but for the time being, he's been granted considerable freedom. My father thinks that travelling will make him a better businessman. Why he turns a blind eye to Otto's main hobbies of boozing and womanising abroad is a mystery to me – as is how Otto manages to attract women in the first place. He's not good-looking – on the small side and stout – and although he's only three years older than me, he looks quite a bit older. I sometimes envy his audacity, conceiving of the world as his for the taking, and mostly getting what he wants, too. I guess it's what you'd call a self-fulfilling prophecy.

I show Sidonie my room, which looks exactly the way I left it a few months ago. She makes herself comfy on the green Empire sofa and watches me unpack. 'Do you think that Jakob will come with Erich?' I ask, and immediately regret it. Talking about men is unchartered territory for us. Apart from that, I suspect that Sidonie is above girls' talk. She shrugs. A knock at the front door saves me. Erich has arrived, without Jakob of course. I'm annoyed at myself.

As always, Mother serves dinner at eight o'clock. My father and Otto have arrived in the meantime. I enjoy big evening meals like these. When I was little, my generous mother would sometimes prevail against my father, and there were times when the neighbours' children, acquaintances and friends all sat together at the long oak table. But then, my father would get the upper hand again. For weeks, my small family sat at the dinner table in silence and I was utterly bored. Then I would long for the old times of talk and commotion, and wished we had a big family. But tonight, it's almost like those lively times again, and everyone's in a good mood. I'm happy we don't say grace before meals: my father always says that you can tell a good Christian by his hard work. My mother has struck up a conversation with Samuel, who is doing his best to remember his table manners. Otto is having a conversation with my father in an overstatedly grown-up tone, which drives me mad. Lore brings in a splendid pork roast, and my heart suddenly sinks: I forgot to tell my parents that I'm a vegetarian now. One after the other, Erich, Samuel and Sidonie politely refuse and help themselves instead to the potato dumplings. I do the same, saying as casually as possible, 'Thank you, I'm a vegetarian.'

My mother stares at me, baffled.

Otto stabs his fork into a piece of meat and says, 'What an interesting excuse to avoid eating pork.'

'What's that supposed to mean?' I say, outraged, although I know exactly what he means.

'Well, your friends here . . . When I was in Kiel last week, the director of the Ironworks group told me that there were never as many Jews in the business as there are now. They've already taken control of the banks, and the entire middle class is next. The Social Democrats just stand by and watch! Just like they did when everything was taken from us. Fehrenbach's government didn't have time to protect German interests in that political chaos!'

'I have no idea what that has to do with Lore's roast, Otto.' My sarcasm fails to sufficiently express my anger. Sidonie studies Otto with an icy stare. My father has got over his astonishment at my new eating habits. Very quietly and very sternly, he says, 'That's enough now, Otto. We do not talk politics at the dinner table.'

Otto immediately obeys: he always obeys my father. An awkward silence follows. As usual, Samuel is more alert than he appears. He saves us by complimenting my mother on the meal.

~

I'm secretly cursing Sidonie. We have had to turn around three times because she's forgotten something. Now we're standing at Charlotte's front door, half an hour later than planned. I know that Charlotte doesn't care about punctuality, especially at her 'soirées', as she calls these parties at her parents' house. But I'm still bothered by Sidonie's notorious lateness. Charlotte throws her arms around me. She is wearing one of her outlandish dresses as usual, the kind that makes me wonder where she does her shopping. Her entire wardrobe is unconventional and every fold of material exudes luxury. She immediately plays the hostess, fetches champagne, points to an enormous mound of food and introduces us to other guests as we pass by. I'm grateful that she accepts my new friends with such ease. They, or we, stand out because of our workers' clothes, Sidonie's trousers and our loose hair lacking pomade or hairclips. Sidonie doesn't care; her expression is even more supercilious than usual, and I'm surprisingly happy to stick out from the crowd with my new friends.

In comparison to my parents' bourgeois flat, Charlotte's place is a grand palace. I'm not even sure what purpose most of the rooms serve. As we enter the *Berliner Zimmer*, the walkthrough room connecting the front and the back of the flat, people are dancing. The slender table in the middle has been pushed aside, with the gramophone on it. Again, I wonder how Charlotte knows all these people. She has closed off the servants' wing and given the staff a day off so that we can 'have the place to ourselves', as she puts it. A tall man wearing a hat pulls her on to the dancefloor. We continue to look around. The three rooms in the front are filled with party guests sitting on sofas or large cushions on the floor. I wave to acquaintances from my school days. From the corner of my eye, I see someone who looks like Jakob; but this is not the first time my imagination has played tricks on me. I'm not going to fall for it again, I think, as Sidonie makes a strange sound and suddenly swoops in his direction. Jakob is sitting on a chaise longue, surrounded by three women and a man, and he smiles up at us, unabashed.

'I was wondering when you were going to show up,' he says. 'When I arrived at Luise's parents' place, you'd already left. And when I arrived here, you hadn't yet turned up. Did you get lost in your own city?' He winks at me and slurps from his champagne flute. I feel annoyed. Why does he think that a smile will make everything better? Then again, what exactly is annoying me? After all, he's under no obligation to let me know of his plans. While I'm still struggling to contain my rage, Sidonie, Erich and Samuel have sat down to join the little group. Sidonie manages to scare off two of the three young ladies by her sheer presence, but one still cleaves to Jakob's side, vying for his attention. The man won't be shooed away either. Jakob flirts with anyone who shows interest in him – male or female, it doesn't seem to matter. I find it confusing even though there are more than a few flamboyant figures in Charlotte's circle of friends. Jakob is wearing a collarless shirt with the sleeves rolled up and has dispensed with a tie, bow-tie or braces, unlike any other man in the room. I suspect he is aware of his boyish good looks and wants to avoid detracting from them in any way. When he enters a room, people pay him the kind of attention usually reserved for beautiful women. This fact – and I have convinced myself over the past few months that it *is* a fact – gives me mixed feelings of resentment and pride.

Charlotte leaves the dancefloor, flops down next to Jakob on the chaise longue and lights a cigarette. 'This young man claims that he's also a student at the Bauhaus,' she says. 'Do you know each other?'

It takes me a moment to grasp her question. 'Charlotte, this is Jakob,' I say.

'This is Jakob? *Your* Jakob? Luise won't shut up about you!' She doesn't bother to whisper. I flush with embarrassment. Charlotte knows very well that nothing but a kiss has passed between Jakob and me; that we're far from being a couple. That I've decided to make a very slow play for him because people like Jakob aren't fond of being pinned down.

'A pleasure,' says Jakob and grins nonchalantly.

Charlotte extends her hand for him to kiss and gives him a delighted smile. Sidonie rolls her eyes. She clearly cannot stand Charlotte, which gratifies me now, but in truth only presents another problem. I can feel the situation slipping out of my grasp.

'I'll get another bottle of champagne,' I say and get up. I struggle through the crowd until I find a fairly quiet spot in the foyer among the coats and handbags that are lying all over the floor. I lean against the wall and close my eyes. To think that I had worried about Charlotte's reactions to the others! Now she's sitting there, flirting with Jakob, making a fool of me and effortlessly winning a face-off with Sidonie. Just as I decide to go home, Samuel appears in front of me. He's holding my handbag, which I must have left behind. Charlotte is wrapping herself in a cashmere scarf, and Sidonie, Erich and Jakob are looking for their coats.

Charlotte says, 'Lu, come on, let's go somewhere else. This party is dying.'

'But how are you going to get rid of all your guests?' I ask, bewildered.

'Oh, they'll find their way out, somehow or other. And

if not,' she replies offhandedly, 'there are enough sofas to sleep on.' Jakob looks at her in admiration. 'A friend of mine is playing the trumpet in a bar on Wielandstraße. Come on, it'll be fun,' says Charlotte. She's already in the stairwell and the others have found their coats at last. With a sigh, I join them.

~

When I wake up, Sidonie has already risen, and my large bed is empty. I hear the sound of clattering plates and a hubbub of voices. I hate people busying about in the mornings! It always sounds like an accusation, a way of reminding late risers like me of all the things we have missed in our sleep. I remain under the covers so no warmth can escape; I lie there and replay last night's events in my mind. The bar that Charlotte dragged us to turned out to be a smoky dive. Her friend, the trumpeter, was nowhere to be seen; instead, the clientele consisted of a couple of old drunkards, a young lady with thick make-up, possibly a prostitute, and two dapper young men whom Charlotte knew. I know she finds those kinds of places exotic. She regards the needy as if they were some thrilling new plaything: I'd never noticed this before. But now that my friends can't even afford the bare essentials, her attitude is off-putting to me. Just as I was ordering a beer from the scowling barman, Jakob and Charlotte suddenly disappeared. The dapper young men were nowhere to be seen either. At first, I thought they had all absconded to the toilet to take drugs because the boys certainly looked as if they indulged in such things. Sidonie sat in the entrance hall and sulked, while Erich, Samuel and I scoured the place for the others. We couldn't find them anywhere. Sidonie wanted to go home, but Erich and Samuel insisted on combing the nearby streets. Exhausted, we finally set off home.

None of this should have come as a surprise, I think, burying my face in the pillow. Seducing handsome men is practically Charlotte's calling. And to count on Jakob's fidelity, which he has never promised me, is ridiculous.

My mother peeks around the door. 'Luise, aren't you hungry? We're all sitting at the breakfast table,' she says.

'I'll be there in a minute!' I reply and reluctantly disentangle myself from the covers.

~

Maria is sitting at the large loom in the furthest corner of the weaving studio. We haven't seen each other since my trip to Berlin. I screw up my courage, roll up a chair and sit down next to her.

'Ah, so Madame deigns to shows her face again?' she says, with a trace of bitterness.

I apologise and quiz her about her latest project until she gradually seems to forget that I've been neglecting her. She even calls me 'Lu' again. The fabric she's weaving is going to be made into cushion covers for a chair prototype that the carpentry workshop has been designing for some weeks.

'If all goes to plan, we can start serial production soon.'

'Do you really want to serialise production? Wouldn't it be much nicer if every chair were unique?' I ask, feeling the fabric.

'Lu, don't even start the "every artwork is an original" discussion again.'

'But where's the problem? No one stands to gain from cheap mass-production.'

'Don't take yourself so seriously as an artist. Technological progress is a fact that even your esoteric nutcases won't be able to get around at some point.'

'Ah, so that's what this is about. Listen, Maria, I'm sorry that we haven't seen much of each other recently. But that's no reason to badmouth my friends.'

Maria goes quiet and fiddles with a new bobbin that she puts into the shuttle. Then she clears her throat and says, 'As you like. I thought you came here to study architecture. If you'd rather paint colourful pictures and dance around in the woods, that's your business.'

'You know very well that there's no department of architecture. You can't blame me for that!'

'Gropius is working with students on the Sommerfeld House. If you weren't so obsessed with your cowl-wearers, you'd have heard about it ages ago.'

This is news to me. I try to come up with an answer when someone behind me says, 'Maria, how are you getting on?' I thought we were alone in the workshop. Embarrassed, I turn and see a young man with blond hair, a wide mouth and deep-set eyes. I know who he is, of course.

'Georg!' Maria's anger seems to evaporate, and her eyes light up. 'If I work hard today and tomorrow, I think we'll be able to start making the covers tomorrow,' she says.

'Don't overdo it,' Georg says and smiles gently. Then he turns to me. 'Georg Muche, I'm master of form at the weaving workshop, have been for a month now. I haven't seen you here before,' he says, reaching out his hand.

'This is Luise,' says Maria. 'She was just on her way out.'

~

I've made myself comfortable on my bed, and spread out the architectural drawings that I submitted for my application. Their technical details are suddenly foreign to me: it's been so long since I last looked at them it's almost like the work of a different person. Maria's words haunt me. Perhaps it's not too late for me to get involved in the Sommerfeld House project? I knew, of course, about plans to create more living quarters for students. People talk a great deal about the lack of space here. But that the actual designs were being made had completely passed me by, even though I would never admit it to Maria.

I wonder who to approach for more information when Frau Werner knocks at my door. 'There's a packet for you, Luise,' she says and hands me a brown paper parcel. I am about to ask who the package is from, but she has already closed the door. The paper is wet from the rain that has been pouring non-stop for weeks. I tear it open and inside there's a coarse brown jacket with a high collar and a pair of loose-fitting trousers – monk's robes! What's more, there's a colourful postcard with a quotation from Hanish:

Greetings and salvation to the hearts that are illuminated by the light of love, and are not guided by the hope of heaven or fear of hell.

Full of excitement, I turn over the card. On the other side, in sweeping handwriting, it says:

Dear Luise,

*We think the time has come to officially welcome you
into our circle. We would be happy if you find the time
to visit us in the House of the Templars on November
17th. We expect to see you there at 6 p.m.*

Yours, Johannes

Yours, Johannes. Not 'Master of Form' or 'Master Itten' –
just 'Johannes'. While the whole package makes me feel
overjoyed, the intimacy of Itten's tone flatters me particularly. Until now, I've only known him as the authoritarian
ruler of the preliminary course. On the few occasions I
might have had the chance to talk to him, I was too intimidated, most probably because of the way the others talk
about him. It's very touching that Erich, Samuel and perhaps even Sidonie have put in a word for me. I don't want
to think about Jakob. I haven't seen him since our trip to
Berlin, and when I do, I am determined to give him the cold
shoulder and disdainful glances.

~

Shortly before six o'clock, I arrive at the House of the
Templars. Although I'm cold and the rain has seeped
through the brown fabric of my new robes, I take a walk
around the building so as not to appear too eager. When I
enter the room, about ten people are standing in a circle
with their eyes closed. Johannes approaches me, takes my
cloak and says softly, 'Over there.' He points to the centre
of the circle. I follow his instructions nervously. Maybe I
wasn't supposed to put on my robes before the initiation?

Erich opens his eyes briefly and flashes me a furtive smile. Then Johannes strikes up a song, and the others join in. Their chanting consists of long, drawn-out syllables in a language I don't understand. I shift from one leg to the other and shiver. The grandeur of the ceremony makes me feel uncomfortable. Everyone having their eyes closed doesn't make it any easier, as if this bizarre ritual had nothing at all to do with me. After what feels like an eternity, the chant ends, and Johannes lays the jacket over my shoulders again. Each person comes over, in turn, to embrace and congratulate me. Even the Mazdaznan followers I don't know say nice things to me.

'About time,' says Jakob and kisses me on the cheek, but really on my mouth. I pull away from his embrace and glare at him. Jakob seems genuinely surprised that I'm angry. Samuel and Erich walk over to me, Samuel skipping and Erich with his usual limp. They present me with a wooden stick, with a sun symbol and an *L* carved in one end.

'For our excursions,' Erich explains, and before he can finish his sentence, Samuel interrupts him impatiently: 'Now you're one of us, you can join in our gymnastics. We go on a long hike once a week.'

Gymnastics! Hiking! The idea is too much for me; in Berlin, I rarely did exercise. On the other hand, it sounds out of the ordinary and exciting; and anyway, I'm touched by the effort the two of them have made.

The cluster of people around me slowly drifts apart. Some say goodbye. Someone has brewed tea, the fire in the hearth has been lit, and I sit down on the carpet next to Erich and Sidonie. Johannes is standing with Jakob in a corner. He has put his arm around Jakob and is talking to him conspiratorially. The two of them almost look like a couple. What an absurd idea. My imagination must be getting the better of me.

'It's good that you came,' says Sidonie, touching my arm with her cool hand, which by her standards is a deeply heartfelt gesture. Since our trip to Berlin, her behaviour towards me in general has changed. She no longer throws me her sceptical looks and addresses me directly. She still keeps her distance, but perhaps this beautiful, inscrutable woman and I will become friends after all.

'Yes, at least one bit of good news this week,' says Erich.

'What's the bad news?' I ask.

'Erich has to move out of his room,' says Sidonie. 'The family he lives with apparently need his room for themselves. But it's only just occurred to them. Narrow-minded liars! They can't stand people being different. They call him "the Galician"' behind his back. But unlike me, Erich isn't even Jewish. And his war service doesn't interest them! Ungrateful bunch!' I have rarely seen Sidonie so riled up.

I don't understand the part about Galicia and the Jews, so I try to nod as sympathetically as possible. 'And where are you going to live now?' I ask Erich.

He shrugs. 'The Prellerhaus is full. Johannes has offered to put me up until I find something new.'

Erich isn't easily rattled, but still, I can feel how worried he is. Then I remember the Sommerfeld House. 'They're planning to build new living quarters for students,' I say. 'Did you know? I'm working on the designs for the building, and when it's finished, I'm sure you'll be able to move in there.' My desire to be useful makes me exaggerate my contribution to the project, as well as its current stage.

Sidonie frowns. 'Do you mean the Sommerfeld House? That's not for students! Gropius is building it for Adolf Sommerfeld, and it's in Berlin. Just a regular commission. Didn't they tell you that?' I'm lost for words and mortified about my bragging.

Erich tries to save me. 'But, Sidonie, aren't there plans to build a Bauhaus housing estate in Weimar, too? That's probably what Luise was talking about.' I don't know any details about this other project but try not to show it.

'Perhaps. But Luise, you're not going to become a handyman, are you? I thought you wanted to make art ... ' Sidonie cocks her head and contemplates me with a look of surprise.

'You know,' I say, 'I'm interested in architecture – I always have been. Does that make me a handyman?'

Sidonie reflects, not so much on my question, I assume, but on whether she wants to confront me. Then Jakob touches my shoulder.

'Luise, shall we go for a walk?' I had wanted to avoid a discussion with Jakob and simply ignore him. But I can't resist his offer and am too curious about what he has to say.

It has stopped raining. We stand in front of the House of the Templars in silence. It seems that Jakob has nothing to say after all. I spot a large sculpture that I have never noticed before. It is a spiral of blue, red and yellow glass fragments, which refract a few weak rays of sunlight. It is both solid and delicate: the glass pieces are set inside curved metal frames whose silvery glare outshines the warm colours. In front of the Gothic building, it has an otherworldly, dazzling effect. Jakob follows my gaze.

'Johannes' latest work. The *Tower of Fire*. Isn't it wonderful?'

'How would I know? I'm not an artist.'

'What makes you say that? Anyway, you don't have to be an artist to be taken by its colours.'

'But colours aren't of any use to anyone. Erich has no roof over his head. And what does Johannes do? He builds wonderful towers that no one can live in.'

Jakob says nothing. Then suddenly: 'Why are you so angry?'

I take a deep breath. I hate being put in the role of the irrational, jealous woman.

'Don't you even realise that we looked everywhere for you in Berlin? We were worried about you. It's not very respectful towards your friends to disappear like that.'

Jakob seems to understand. 'I wasn't with Charlotte, in case that's what you're thinking.'

I wait, but he doesn't seem inclined to explain himself any further. The silence between us grows heavier and my anger coils up inside me, like the stupid spirals I am still staring at. It takes all my willpower not to ask Jakob any more questions. Eventually, I say, 'It's starting to rain again. I think I'd better go home.' Jakob does not attempt to stop me, and after I've walked a few yards, tears well up in my eyes. When I reach Frau Werner's garden gate, I realise I haven't said goodbye to the others.

~

I lost sight of our hiking group a while ago. Only Samuel has fallen behind, to keep me and hobbling Erich company. They have brought the walking stick that I left behind at the House of the Templars after my hasty departure. Supposedly, we have been lucky with the weather. To me, it just seems like another one of those grey days when it's hard to tell whether dusk has already fallen. We've been walking to Ettersberg Ridge since the morning. I'm out of breath, and secretly wonder if I can leave my walking stick behind without them noticing.

'Where are we going anyway?' I ask Erich, puffing.

'We're not going anywhere in particular. We're just taking a walk in the countryside.'

His statement is not very satisfying, and it must show because, after a while, Erich says good-naturedly: 'I know it's not easy to go along with these things. But try. It's worth it, I promise.'

The path we're on turns into a beaten track, and it gets steeper all the time. Just as I'm about to give in to my bad mood and sit down on the next rock like a small child, refusing to go on, the path flattens out. Sparse beech trees line the track to form a high, leafless wall. We're completely alone; no one says anything and the only sound is the trees creaking in the wind. Then we reach a small clearing. The others are already sitting in a circle. In the distance, I can make out a large building, perhaps a castle. Hopefully, it's not our journey's destination. We have to walk back the whole way, too, after all.

Johannes is barefoot. He's sitting on a large stone, his long legs intertwined in a complicated pose. Although his eyes are closed, he seems to take in everything that is going on around him. 'So, now we are all here,' he says. We sit down with the others in the damp grass. 'Let's begin in a cross-legged position with our hands in front of our hearts. Now that we have cleansed our bodies, we shall do the same for our souls,' Johannes says. 'Close your eyes and empty your heads.' I try to follow his instructions, but fall at the first hurdle: I can't empty my head. I don't know how to think of nothing at all. Thinking doesn't consist of individual words – thoughts are too fast for that. It has become very quiet, I can only hear the others breathing. Jakob is conspicuous once again by his absence. It seems that all the teachers have curtailed their expectations of him and his dutifulness. His talent seems sufficient to make him a constant exception. As if not everyone here was talented. Finally, there are more instructions.

'Allow all your muscles to relax. Now, slowly fill your lungs without straining. Hold your breath for a few seconds. Just exhale a little and then stop breathing again. Continue until all the breath in your lungs empties.' We repeat the whole thing five times until I start to hyperventilate. Johannes says: 'Now let's finish the exercise with the sacred vowel "O".'

Everyone strikes up the drawn-out syllable at a different pitch: it sounds so off-key that I can barely hold back my laughter. And still it's annoying to not understand it all. You only need to look at Johannes to see that these exercises are effective. He is fully in control of his body. Asceticism doesn't require any effort on his part. Despite his sternness, he doesn't come across as austere, but serious and alert.

An aura of calm emanates from him. And the others look calmer too now, or at least they seem so to me.

Then we set off downhill, homeward this time. Someone starts singing a song, an old hiking tune, which I can join in with for once. Samuel takes my hand, and we end up skipping more than walking. When we reach the slope, some flop down into the grass. The high spirits prove infectious and soon, ten of us are rolling down the hill. Laughing and breathless, I lie at the bottom and wait for the world to stop spinning.

We walk back along the narrow path to town. I'm cold, and the thought of the fireplace in the House of the Templars spurs me on. I join a smaller group who are at the front, including Sidonie. The others have fallen behind, probably to snatch a coveted private conversation with Johannes. Sidonie is back to pretending that we hardly know each other. She ignores my contributions to the conversation. At some point I give up, frustrated, and carry on walking in silence beside her. By now it's afternoon and already dark; the yellow gas lamps of Weimar glimmer in the distance. As we enter town, we run into a group of men. They say something I don't catch. I greet them as we pass.

'Whores!', 'Think they're so modern!' I hear them say behind me, much nearer than I expected. Only then do I realise that the men are following us. There are four of us, all women. 'You're not from the Bauhaus. You're from the whorehouse!' one harangues us. The others jeer and laugh.

We walk faster. Sidonie's eyes flash, but she clearly can't think of a way out. Two of the men walk past us and block our path while the others stand behind us.

'We could teach these pretty things a lesson on morals and decency,' one says.

Sidonie can no longer contain herself. 'And you think this is decent? Harassing girls on the street?' The tallest man takes a step towards her. In a panic, I try to get a grip on myself, but my mind has shut down. I don't know what to do.

'Good evening, gentlemen, can I help you?' Johannes calls out from a distance. I laugh involuntarily. The arrival of the large group swiftly changes the situation. The men retreat into a side alley. Johannes gently touches my arm and my paralysis slowly subsides. We walk the rest of the way swiftly, without talking.

~

The run-up to Christmas passes quickly, in a general whirl of activity. I haven't been able to find out much more about the Sommerfeld House or housing estate plans but my days are busy all the same. Erich has dug out a Mazdaznan brochure with instructions for the cold season, which I've been conscientiously studying. I do my daily exercises, take cold baths and drink hot brews made of grains and fruit. I can't say whether I'm any closer to attaining a state of transcendence, but I do feel healthy. Having an organising principle in my life feels good. Nearly everyone else has broken the autumn fast again, and I've made up my mind to join in the next time. Although I'm finding it difficult to adjust to the new eating habits, it's probably just a question of practice and discipline. I'm now more than halfway through the preliminary course and in spring, the decision will be made whether I'm allowed to stay at the Bauhaus.

'It depends whether you're taken on by a workshop. But with your material-intellectual temperament, that won't be a problem. Don't think about it too much,' Erich says one evening in the canteen. It helps that my friends are a semester ahead of me, but I still feel as if I'm lagging. The division of temperaments, mostly based on the shapes of our skulls, still feels quite alien to me but I appreciate Erich's encouragement. I look up at the boarded ceiling and regret, as I always do when I sit here, that the windows are missing. Ashen December sunlight falls through the chinks in the planks. The dining room isn't heated, so we're huddled close together, sharing one prickly blanket that Samuel has brought 'so that we don't catch a cold'.

Sidonie says, 'If I were you, I'd join the weaving workshop. Johannes had to give up as workshop master this year, but Muche isn't bad. You'd have a fair amount of artistic freedom.'

In the beginning, I found Sidonie's mercurial affections very confusing. But I've got used to it. Even though there's no apparent logic to her moods, I've decided to treat them like changes in the weather or seasons. Just as I'm about to ignore her comment and explain that the carpentry workshop is the only place where I can train to be an architect, Jakob opens the door. He pulls up a stool and sits on it, legs apart, facing us.

'Oh, a feast!' he says, eyeing our plates. His cheeks are flushed and he's in excellent spirits. It's been so long since I saw him that I grin at him unintentionally.

'Well,' I say, 'we have to make sure that we're getting our intake of onions and garlic.' Cooking vegetarian food on a non-existent budget and getting it to taste good is not proving easy for the cooks, who solve the problem by throwing a few too many cloves in the pot.

'No need to be so prissy,' Sidonie says. Jakob grins at me, rolling his eyes in a way that eludes her. 'Have you heard? There's even a vote being passed around, for or against onions. But it's just another attempt to sabotage us,' Sidonie says, fuming.

Jakob says: 'Samuel, why don't you cook for us? We all know that you're a born mother.'

Samuel laughs good-naturedly and sets his glasses straight, the way he always does when he's teased. I can't swallow a bite in Jakob's presence, even though I'm hungry.

'How's it going in sculpture class?' Sidonie asks Jakob.

'Johannes is still teaching us. But the constant personnel changes are a bit bizarre. How are we supposed to work in peace when new masters keep taking over?'

'I think it's because Gropius got cold feet at some point. Johannes has been the head of nearly all the workshops. Gropius is always making a show of being friendly – but he's power-conscious too,' Sidonie says, looking at her plate with a dark expression.

'I don't know. We shouldn't always assume the worst. Perhaps Johannes can concentrate better on his art if he doesn't have to run all the workshops. The new master of form in mural painting is Oskar Schlemmer, and he's almost always there,' says Erich.

'That's right. I talked to Johannes about him yesterday,' says Jakob. 'He's relieved.'

Jakob's familiar tone when talking about Johannes makes me uneasy, but I don't know why. 'I'm off,' says Jakob, standing up. 'I wanted to go over the details of my new work with him this evening. Goodbye, dear Mazdaznan brothers!'

Whenever he turns up out of the blue and then disappears just as quickly, I feel like someone who has fallen for the same card trick over and over again.

~

I stand in front of the door of the carpentry workshop, hesitating. There's just a week to go until the Julklapp festival, the last festivity of the year. It's taking place at Gropius' flat. Everyone is supposed to buy a small gift, which is assigned at random to another guest. It's not that easy to choose a suitable present, quite aside from the fact that the only shop I regularly visit in Weimar is the small kiosk on Seifengasse.

Three older students are standing at different workbenches and don't even look up when I enter. My brilliant idea fades a little. I was going to carve something in the carpentry workshop and while doing so, find out which students are working on architectural projects. But no one here is carving anything: I should have realised that, but I was too busy trying to find out who the workshop master was. Carving is done in the wood sculpture workshop, of course. But they don't work on architectural projects there. So, I try not to let it show that I've never been here before and walk purposefully over to a crate filled with large pieces of wood in different sizes. I don't know what I want to make, or how to do it exactly. Small, I think: the smaller, the easier. I pick out a fist-sized block of wood and look around the room for some tools. Saws, planes and chisels, all marked with initials, hang in neat rows on the wall. I stare at the equipment uncertainly: I've already poached some wood; I can't just take away another student's tools. The three young men continue to ignore me. Well then, worst-case scenario, I'll have to apologise and give everything back. I pick out the smallest chisel and the tiniest of hammers.

I had the vague notion of chiselling a little jewellery box. But that would take too long, and anyway, I know that I'm not skilled enough. You can never go wrong with the three basic geometric shapes. My piece of wood is already square; I doubt I can make a triangle, so, a circle it is, a well-formed, polished sphere. I go over to the workbench where a red-haired boy is sawing non-stop on a piece of teak wood, making quite a racket. The longer I work on my piece of wood, the smaller it gets. I keep finding areas that are too angular or too flat. It starts to get difficult to hold the object in the metal vice. I put my tools down and look around for help. The red-haired boy continues to ignore me. Then the other two approach him, spread a plan out on the table, and he stops working on his piece for a moment.

'If we leave the door in the centre, we're going to have problems with the stairs,' the smaller of the two says. 'Even if we make the tread smaller, you'll hardly be able to get past the banister.'

The plan is lying upside down very near to me, and I try to make out what's on it. I see a drawing of a staircase.

'The door has to stay in the centre. But we could make it a few centimetres smaller,' says the redhead, blinking.

'We can't. The others finished the door a week ago,' says the taller one, who's wearing a strange cap. By now, I think I've worked out what the problem might be. And how to solve it.

'And what if we make the room slightly bigger?' suggests the redhead.

The other two shake their heads again. 'Then the ceiling span will be too wide.'

I become agitated. 'Have you thought about introducing the banister from the second step up?'

The three boys look up at me in surprise. My heart starts hammering. Perhaps I shouldn't have said anything, but the solution seems so obvious.

'From the second step up? How would that look?' the redhead says.

'Yeah, that only makes everything even more complicated,' says the small guy, shaking his head.

'*I*'ve got it!' says the cap-wearer. 'We could turn the first step into a podium. Then we don't have to adjust the rise. Like this,' he says and scribbles something on the plan.

The other two are delighted; the redhead slaps him on the shoulder in admiration. But that's exactly what I said. Angrily, I turn back to my uneven – and now tiny – sphere, deciding to sand it off so that I can leave as soon as possible.

~

The Christmas party is already in full swing when Samuel and I arrive at Gropius' flat. I'm relieved I didn't have to come alone. Samuel has become my confidante over the past few weeks, especially concerning Jakob. I can't speak to Charlotte about him any more. I've tried talking to her about the weekend in Berlin; she hotly denies being interested in him. Still, I avoid answering her questions about my love life in our letters. Maria, my former confidante, doesn't visit me any more. The rare conversations we have in the corridors or canteen are like stiff, polite dances around certain subjects. So now it's Samuel who's forced to listen to the details of my almost non-existent affair with Jakob. In return, I put up with endless accounts about his physical condition. Samuel is always suffering from some ailment, which he has to analyse in minute detail. But still, I am surprised how keen he is on analysing the maze of Jakob's mind.

'He's sure to be here too!' he whispers now, pulling me in by the hand.

The mood is cheerfully chaotic. The students are scattered throughout the flat, standing in the kitchen, sitting on the floor in the living room, and so tightly packed into the hallway that we can barely squeeze past. A chubby student with a canvas sack in his hand shouts, 'Presents over here!' I'd rather pretend that I've forgotten to bring something. But instead, I wait patiently while the boy writes a number on my sculpted sphere wrapped in newspaper and puts it in his sack.

Samuel brings us juice, potatoes and beetroot from the grand buffet, which is probably also decked with precious hams and roasts. Then we go straight over to the corner where Erich and Jakob are sitting on the floor. We talk about the holidays.

'Are you sure you don't want to come with me to my parents' place?' Samuel gives Jakob a fond look.

'I'd love to, but I can't leave my mother on her own. Johannes has already given me the train fare,' says Jakob. 'And anyway, Erich's coming with you, isn't he? Won't your house be too crowded?'

'Oh, our place is always full. You know what my family is like. And anyway, we're going to our country house, which has more room than the city flat. You're very welcome,' Samuel says. But Jakob has already decided.

I realise that I know almost nothing about my friends' families. It's a strange result of us living together in a microcosm of our own making.

'You're not going home, Erich?' I ask above the hubbub of voices.

'No,' says Erich quietly.

The sudden hush among us makes me uncomfortable. Samuel, who can always be relied upon in such circumstances, stands up and says to Erich, 'I feel strange; my stomach is acting up again. Come on, let's see if they have any tea.'

Now I'm on my own with Jakob. He's unusually attentive, refills my drink and asks about my plans for the coming year. He explains to me that Erich's parents are strict Catholics and pinned all their hopes on their only son. They already frowned upon his decision to study at the Bauhaus, but when he turned up last year at the Viennese family home in monk's robes, following obscure Far Eastern traditions, their patience ran out. 'Erich misses his parents very much,' Jakob says. 'I miss my father too.'

Jakob's father never returned from the war. I listen to him for a long time. He talks about how his mother still believes his father is missing in action and is bound to come home sooner or later. He tells me that he was certain his father was dead when he hadn't returned two weeks after the war ended. But that he still combed the public offices and administration agencies for a long time to give his mother the same feeling of certainty. The way he talks about his mother moves me. His sudden vulnerability is endearing. Handsome, mysterious Jakob, who usually hides behind a coquettish mask, revealing himself to me, of all people. Our closeness, the hot punch and the sudden significance of things at the end of the year, create a tension between us that overwhelms me. When he finally kisses me, the presents are already being handed out. Numbers are shouted around the room; packages pass hands. No one takes any notice of us. This kiss is very different from our first hasty kiss in the summer. It lasts. It has purpose.

'I'd like to take you somewhere else.' The shyness in Jakob's voice surprises me. My head crowds with voices. Most insist that I mustn't go anywhere with Jakob, not on any account. An unmarried girl of my age with no securities – what if people talk? I shudder, thinking of my mother. No matter what, there would surely be consequences for me, especially with a man famous for his elusiveness. I think of Charlotte. She has never suffered any consequences. She dismisses gossip with a casual flick of her hand, just like her admirers' countless marriage proposals. And if I'm honest, it wasn't hard to forget that awkward boy I once succumbed to on Charlotte's sofa.

Jakob kisses me again, and another voice mingles with the crowd in my head. I don't want to stay here where everyone can watch us and where we will eventually have to part. I want to get even closer to him. *Why should I deny myself this?* adds the defiant new voice. I do a quick assessment: Frau Werner is a deep sleeper and to get to my room, we only have to cross the hallway. The defiant voice wins. 'We can go to mine,' I say quietly.

During the long walk to my place, we don't talk, not because we feel awkward, but because every word would mean risking our desire.

We sleep together with great care and concentration, but without words. We only make brief eye contact as if we don't want to acknowledge the intimacy we're sharing. I don't open my eyes until Jakob comes. The tension between us uncoils, and he holds me in his arms and smiles, still breathless.

Hours later, I'm still wide awake. Now and again, I open my eyes to make sure that it's really Jakob asleep next to me. The scale of the events on this one evening makes me nervous, euphoric, almost dizzy. I move as little as possible so that I don't wake him. To try to calm down, I stare at the sharp contours of the shadows thrown on to the ceiling by the insipid light coming from the street lamp. Time becomes amorphous. I feel for my wristwatch on the floor next to the bed. It's four o'clock in the morning.

Jakob wakes up. 'I have to go,' he whispers.

'Why? Frau Werner never comes in to my room in the morning, and as soon as she's out in the garden, I can smuggle you out of the front door.'

I don't want him to leave. It seems unfair – downright tragic – that our night together should already be over.

'The family I live with will wonder where I am. And besides, Hanish says in winter, people should only spend half the night together in one bed.'

Hanish! Hanish has no business in my bedroom. But I don't want to nag him, so I say nothing. Jakob gives me a fleeting kiss.

'See you tomorrow, beautiful,' he says, which mollifies me. He shuts the door softly. I listen to his footsteps; then it all goes quiet.

~

When I stumble into the kitchen the following day, I feel my body is sorely lacking sleep. The house is quiet: it's Sunday, and Frau Werner is probably at church. I'm glad she's not here so that I can let my thoughts run free. My mind is doing somersaults, blanking out Hanish and my disappointment at the abrupt end to our night together, replaying each moment. I juggle the images into a hierarchy: the more precious the moment, the less often I repeat it in my head.

Sitting at the breakfast table, a feeling of having forgotten something suddenly hits me. An exercise for the preliminary course? Something I was supposed to get for my family before Christmas? I already have presents for everyone, including Charlotte. I want to tell her about my night with Jakob. Then it dawns on me. Charlotte once showed me how to douche with vinegar as a contraceptive.

'The only important thing is that you do it straight afterwards,' she drummed into me. I panic. I hadn't thought of that at all.

Phone Charlotte, I think. She'll know what to do. But as

far as I know, there are only two telephones at the Bauhaus: one is the director's and the other, the secretary's. In emergencies, students are allowed to use the secretary's phone, but I can't risk someone hearing me. A letter would take far too long. Maria won't be able to help me, and I don't want to ask Sidonie either – if only I could talk to Charlotte! I stare at the piece of bread lying untouched on my plate, and the solution comes to me in a flash – a telegram! I leave everything as it is, hastily pull on my coat and run out along the park towards the centre of town. I slip a few times because the ground is icy.

Despite the cold, I feel warm when I arrive breathlessly at the post office. It's closed, of course. It is still Sunday, after all. Slowly, I trudge home and decide to try again tomorrow. To distract myself from feeling panicked, I plan the following day in minute detail, even down to the wording of the telegram. 'Call me – urgent – Luise.' That will do, but what number is she supposed to call me on? It's no use, I'll have to wait. In a week I'll be going to my parents for Christmas anyway, and then I can interrogate Charlotte.

When I arrive home, Frau Werner hasn't yet returned. I can't stand waiting around and doing nothing, so I decide to do the douche anyway. In the pantry, I find apple vinegar, then I warm a pan of water and take the mixture in a bowl up to the bathroom. Perhaps a few hours won't make a difference. Although it's not his fault, I curse Jakob, who is probably strolling around Weimar at this very moment, without a care in the world.

～

When I finally manage to talk to Charlotte between Christmas and New Year's Eve, my conversation with her is anything but reassuring. No, she says blithely, she can't think of anything to prevent an unwanted pregnancy at this stage. But rather than dwelling on it, she congratulates me on my conquest and wants to hear all the details. I tell her what happened but not without checking that Jakob's disappearance in Berlin had nothing to do with her. At last, I'm the one who has something to tell. We spend a long time talking that evening, and I remember what I like about Charlotte: she isn't judgemental, listens for hours and manages to see the funny side of even the most dire situations.

I'm queasy with fear that my mother will notice a change in me, and it doesn't stop until New Year's Eve. On that morning, to my great relief, my period starts. Now I regret skulking about the flat in a depressed mood for a week, despite the festivity of the decorations by my family's strait-laced standards. My father has been distracted but not unfriendly; my mother has spoiled me and hasn't asked many questions. Not even Otto has been around to bother me: he is away on business. The quiet celebrations, the sanctioned idleness, the lavish evening meal – I could have enjoyed it all. Instead, I spent most of the time up in my room, pretending to read and staring at the ceiling.

Charlotte holds her annual New Year's Eve party. I stand around missing my friends. While an excited young man talks to me about some new theatre production, I work out the details of my next rendezvous with Jakob. And when

1922 is ushered in with great jubilation, I conjure up various scenarios for my future love life. My personal romance novel becomes more and more outlandish but always has a happy ending, in keeping with the genre.

~

Weimar seems just as small and decorative as it did last summer when I stood outside Frau Werner's door for the first time. I still haven't got used to the contrast between these fanciful cottages and gardens and the huge apartment buildings and boulevards of Berlin. My hands are clammy as I put down my case to unlock the door. Frau Werner has clearly been waiting for me: she comes towards me down the hallway, then takes a note from the small living-room table and squeezes it into my hand with an overfamiliar wink. 'Have you already bagged yourself an admirer, Luise?'

I am so hopeful that the note is from Jakob that I don't even take the time to blush. However, it seems highly unlikely that my love story has already gone a step towards becoming reality. I don't read the message straight away. Instead, I put it on my dresser and unpack my things very carefully while, out of the corner of my eye, the letter seems to loom. Only once I've put everything away and can't think of anything else to delay the moment, I unfold it. 'Luise! Movies? Jakob' is what it says. I hardly pay attention to its brevity and look tenderly for a long time at the exclamation mark, which seems to hold a particular significance.

~

Jakob picks me up, and we stroll through the park into the centre of town. It took weeks for what was written on his note to translate into action. He kept putting me off at the last moment until I was sure that he'd had second thoughts. I saw him in passing a few times, and on those occasions, I tried to seem as nonchalant as possible. Now I'm chattering away nervously and laughing too much, but it doesn't seem to bother him. He fools around, jostles me playfully and at some point, even takes me by the hand. Everything about him seems carefree: his trousers that hang a little too low, his unbuttoned monk's robe with its stiff collar, even the curls that fall on to his face. When we reach Frauenplan, we see Maria coming from the other direction. She is either in a hurry or pretending to be. In any case, before I can introduce her to Jakob, she has already walked past. It still hurts that our friendship has fallen apart, and I resolve to visit her. It starts drizzling. I link arms with Jakob, and he touches my hand. Weimar is small, and I often run into people I know when out walking. I'm still surprised to see Samuel coming towards us. From afar, he gives me a conspiratorial grin; after all, he has suffered with me through every one of Jakob's promises and cancellations. Jakob spots Samuel too and pulls his arm away from me. 'Samuel! We were just on our way to the picture house. Care to join us?'

I can't believe my ears. And there I was thinking that we were on a date. Unfortunately, Samuel says much too quickly, 'Sure! I haven't been in ages.' After all those evenings I spent with him, spinning out my romantic woes, I expect a little more loyalty from him. What's even more

annoying is the way that Jakob avoids any physical contact with me from then on.

The picture house is showing *Nosferatu*. I vaguely remember Charlotte telling me she'd seen the première in the Marmorsaal cinema. But this is not Berlin. The cramped room barely seats forty. The hard chairs have probably been cobbled together from various businesses, and the musical accompaniment is played by a pitiful band of three men who are huddled next to the piano — no match for the splendour of the Filmpalast at Zoologischer Garten, where my mother has sometimes taken me.

The weekly newsreel covers the story of Reichskanzler Wirth's press conference about the Treaty of Rapallo and is loudly commented on from all sides. The screen shows a flickering headline: 'Wirth explains: The Treaty has been published in full and contains no secret agreements of a political or military character.' In the front row, there is mocking laughter. 'Who believes that!' 'The media's in on it, too!' Jakob hums absently to himself.

'A peace treaty is no reason to get paranoid,' I argue, not quite under my breath. A sluggish man in the front row is about to object when the music announces the beginning of the film.

Jakob takes my hand again but in such a way so Samuel won't see. I try not to look at Jakob's profile. Then I get engrossed in the film. It draws me in so much that I'm almost embarrassed. Estate agent Knock is creepy enough, but when Count Orlok appears, I'm terrified. I'm relieved when the closing credits roll. Jakob suggests we make an exception and go to the pub next to the picture house. I desperately

hope that Samuel will understand the situation and go home. Neither of them can afford a drink and normally Samuel says that beer only aggravates his never-ending digestive problems. But my hopes are crushed: he sticks around.

The pub is deserted except for two figures sitting silently at the bar. When I comment on this, the bartender shrugs and simply says: 'Everyone's broke.' To his disappointment, we just order tea.

'Wasn't it fantastic how the film connected the supernatural and the natural?' Jakob asks us. His pathos and enthusiasm, which I admired a few months ago, suddenly grate on my nerves.

I just found the film scary, so I say nothing. But Samuel picks up on Jakob's enthusiasm. 'Yes, and all those nature themes! The animals knew what was going on,' he says.

'The link to the occult was really clear. That letter at the beginning – those were Cabbalist signs, right?'

A discussion unfolds as to whether film is a Dionysian or an Apollonian medium. I've just finished reading *The Birth of Tragedy* and don't feel like getting involved. I don't know whether Nietzsche's criteria can even be applied to the medium of film. Doubts always surface in me whenever I listen to my friends talking. It's enlightening, even liberating sometimes, that they believe life is unpredictable, but I can't accept that everything is completely random. Apart from that, I'd rather have talked about the peace treaty, but neither of the two seems the least bit interested.

I drift off and think how outrageous it is that Samuel has stolen my evening with Jakob, just like that. I shiver, more from exhaustion and exasperation than from cold. Samuel

immediately comes to my aid: 'Luise, are you cold? Would you like my jacket?'

'No, thank you. Do you always have to play the Good Samaritan?'

Jakob looks at me in surprise and says: 'Luise, Samuel was just trying to help. That's no reason to have a go at him.'

He talks to me as if reproving a small child. I feel incapable of snapping out of my mood, so I say: 'Well, now there's two good Samaritans. I hope you get along. Enjoy your evening.'

I try to leave the pub in a suitably dramatic fashion, but the corner of my coat gets caught on the door handle. Filled with shame and anger, I walk around the narrow streets until I suddenly find myself standing in front of the building where Maria lives. The thought of her warm-hearted, throaty laugh suddenly seems very comforting. Without thinking about it much, I take the old familiar route through the separate entrance door, up the steps to the fourth floor, along the low-ceilinged corridor, until I am standing in front of Maria's room. After knocking, I don't hear anything for a long time; then there's a rustling sound, and Maria opens the door. She looks surprised. And why wouldn't she? I haven't visited her in months. Coming here wasn't such a great idea after all, considering my jittery state.

'What are you doing here?' She doesn't sound particularly friendly.

'I just wanted ... when I saw you earlier on I ... it's such a shame that we don't see each other any more and I thought ... ' I stammer.

Her face brightens a little.

'Come in. You look completely frozen.'

Her horrid roommate isn't around for once. We sit down on the narrow bed, which is covered in a grey blanket.

'Lu, you look terrible. What happened?'

Her empathy only makes things worse. 'Jakob—' I burst out but don't get any further because I am crying so hard.

Maria strokes my shoulder and makes soothing noises, but I envision a smile on her lips.

'I've always told you that they're not good people. And that pretty boy is the worst.'

I shouldn't have said anything. But Maria's arm around my shoulder feels good, as does railing about Jakob. I tell Maria about our evening, but even while I do, I realise how unreasonable it was to storm out.

'Don't worry about it, Luise. I'm not even sure Jakob is into women, to be honest,' she says.

'What do you mean?'

Maria is still smiling, conspiratorially now.

'Of course, they're just rumours, but people say that's he's very close to Master Itten, if you know what I mean.'

I don't understand a thing. I don't *want* to understand. Jakob and Johannes: impossible. But then again, the long periods he spends with Johannes, the familiar way he says his name. But why would he get involved with me? I say the last sentence out loud.

Maria says: 'Maybe it's not even true. But if there's any truth in it, Jakob would need an "official" girlfriend.'

'Official! If only! Jakob hides me whenever anyone else turns up.'

'Maybe he's not sure himself. In any case, I'd be careful.'

We carry on speculating about Jakob's motives for a long time, and the evening rebuilds the closeness between Maria and me, even though I suspect that it won't last long.

~

I am nervous. In the bright room on the third floor where we normally have lessons, we are presenting our preliminary course work. An assessment committee led by Johannes walks through the room. The teachers stop at every student, talk to each one about his or her work, and then recommend which workshop they should join. Johannes' recommendations are rarely contradicted. Soon it'll be my turn. Right now, the small group of masters has reached the slender boy next to me, who is leaning forward slightly to show a detail on the lower edge of his big wood and metal sculpture, which looks alarmingly militaristic.

I can't concentrate on what he's saying. My fragile wooden construction is standing on a plinth that I made especially for it. I'm worried that it's as fragile it looks. Over the past two weeks, I have been working in the carpentry workshop non-stop so that I can show something from the preliminary course that's more representative of my interests. At first, the students there were suspicious of me, but then I made an arrangement with the master of form and they got used to my presence. After a while, they even praised my skills, and when I eventually finished, they all admired my sculpture. It's not very tall, just about knee-height, and is an assembly of finely chiselled pieces of wood, held together by threads and strings, an architectural model not intended to be realised. It's supposed to look delicate, floating, and at the same time technical, like the palimpsest of a drawing.

Now it's my turn, and although I have thought very carefully about what I am going to say, my body suddenly sabotages me. I hear a humming sound in my ears, I start to sweat profusely, and my heart hammers so loudly that I blurt out my words. What's worse, Johannes asks me all these questions that have nothing to do with my sculpture. I simply don't get around to explaining my imaginary building. The fact that Johannes doesn't seem to understand only adds to my frustration.

Finally, I hear him say: 'Don't worry, Luise. Most women are deficient in three-dimensional visualisation. It has nothing to do with you. But I would recommend you join the textile workshop. There you can develop your talent for colour schemes, which you have already proven.'

I look at him with animosity but say nothing. It's only when the committee has moved on to the next girl that the implications of his verdict hit me with full force. I won't be allowed to join the carpentry workshop; instead, I'll be made to sit in the weaving workshop with Maria and Sidonie and do something that hasn't the slightest relevance to construction. All those weeks I spent working on my sculpture have been wasted, not to mention the countless magazines I've read to develop a better understanding of contemporary architectural theories. My disappointment is difficult to bear. I'm furious at my naïvety. I never even doubted that I would be allowed to join the carpentry workshop. And then a thought crosses my mind that upsets me even more: what if Johannes is right? Perhaps I do lack the talent. I think back with horror to my first encounter with

Gropius. Even then he was probably trying to gently hint that I wasn't suited to architecture, and I was too deluded to admit it.

~

I spend the holidays almost exclusively up in my room. So soon after Christmas, no one feels it is worth going home. To avoid thinking about Jakob, Johannes and the impending weaving workshop, I bury myself in books. I am tired of standing around among my friends like a distant observer. I want to finally belong. It's not as if anyone has been stopping me. Even Sidonie has accepted me at this point. But I have my doubts about the teachings of Mazdaznan, which make me feel vaguely deceitful. My friends are intelligent people, and I have the greatest respect for Johannes. There must be something that I haven't yet understood.

I have borrowed all the library books whose titles or authors I have heard of from friends. Now they lie piled on my dresser: an off-puttingly thick book called *The Great Initiates*, a novel by Knut Hamsun, African fairy tales and, lastly, *The Book of the Way and its Virtue* by Lao Tzu. I also have a few back copies of *Der Sturm*. I start with the novel but find the endless descriptions of nature tiresome, and the hero is so disagreeable that I soon lose patience. I flick through the magazines instead. I read a few interesting articles on art history, which don't give me the feeling of having got very far in my search for answers.

Then my gaze falls on a small book with the title *The Dissolution of Cities*. I borrowed it because I'd already heard the name of the author, Bruno Taut, in connection with

Gropius. The book consists almost entirely of illustrations and panels of images, with very little accompanying text. I am immediately engrossed. Finally I am encountering an architectural vision that not even Sidonie would dismiss with a smirk. She always acts as if construction were merely the job of workmen, not worthy of artistic ambitions. But Taut's vision is the end of cities, of communities in nature in which people live without fences. There is nothing in it that contradicts the teachings of Mazdaznan. Quite the contrary: there are a few temples, such as the 'Shrine of the Incandescent', stretching up like a flame, and the 'Temple of Stars', which really is star-shaped but looks more like a plant. Technology plays a role in his designs, too. 'The Great Flower', for example, is a kind of fertility symbol as well as being a way of guiding air traffic. But high up in the corner, it says almost demonstratively: 'Technology is very different from the factory-chimney Stone Age.' The drawings are rough sketches rather than detailed plans, apparently to emphasise the organic nature of the forms. If architecture can look like this, then perhaps there is a place for me in Mazdaznan's worldview after all.

I laugh at the tilting phallus, which presumably blinks to guide in aeroplanes. At that point, I spot a sentence scribbled in the bottom corner that I'd almost overlooked: 'The concept of property has disappeared and, consequently, so has marriage. Everything is "borrowed goods". Pleasure is only joy.' I think of Jakob. I have never even hinted at marriage, but perhaps I've approached it all the wrong way. I know that you can't own a person. I don't even see myself as someone who aspires to that. But I have to admit that the way

I've behaved towards him has been just that: possessive. My gnawing jealousy, which has dulled into a constant wrenching feeling, disappears all of a sudden. Perhaps the key to dealing with Jakob lies somewhere in Bruno Taut's sentence. Maybe I have to drum this truth into my head until it finally sinks in. I put the book aside and go in search of Jakob.

I find him in the sculpture workshop. He's amazed to see me, and only then do I realise that I have no idea what I want to say to him. Instead of telling him about my new way of seeing things, I start up a friendly, superficial conversation. I get the feeling he doesn't really want to know why I'm not angry with him any more. With a casualness I didn't know I could muster, and which I greatly prefer to the uptight scepticism that's been weighing me down for weeks, I say goodbye soon afterwards – but not without kissing him on the cheek.

~

Encouraged by my earlier reading, I decide to be a little stricter with myself, even as far as my body is concerned. Up until now, I've followed the teachings of our lifestyle in a half-hearted way. Although I've stopped eating meat, take alternately hot and cold baths, and go on hikes, I gave up getting up at dawn after two days. I have never studied the doctrine of temperament to join in the speculations about other students' characters with my friends, and I've never fasted.

Now I'm determined to put aside the last remnants of doubt that are still drifting through my mind. The others have already been fasting for about a week, but Erich has reassured me that even a short phase can purify the body.

I usually turn to Erich when I have questions about the teachings. In contrast to Sidonie, who merely raises her eyebrows, and Jakob, who I still want to impress, he explains everything to me gently and patiently. He never acts like I should know all this already.

He gives me a bitter tincture to use as a laxative. The first three days are terrible: but Erich warned me about this. I have stomach cramps and can't sleep, but most of all, I can't focus on anything but the emptiness in my head. Maybe this is the whole point of the exercise, but I feel bored. Time has never passed so slowly. I dutifully get up at dawn, which always feels like it is the middle of the night. Being hungry makes me even more tired, and so I stumble through the day, barely able to talk to people. I try to stick to the prescribed physical exercises, but during the first long walk, I become so jittery that I have to turn back. If I had the energy, I'd probably be furious: who thinks up such things at a time when no one has enough to eat in the first place?

On the fourth day of fasting I wake up and everything has changed. My senses are so sharp that I can smell Frau Werner's coffee down in the kitchen all the way up in my room. Everything is more colourful than usual, and I feel a sense of wild euphoria. The feeling of transparency, unpleasant the day before, has changed into a light, floating sensation. For the first time in days, I want to be with other people and talk.

For the rest of the fasting period, I spend the days in the House of the Templars, where Erich now unofficially lives. Going on walks isn't difficult any more. In the morning, we do gymnastics, and at midday and in the evening, we stroll through the park. Even though I would never admit it, I feel morally superior to the other students, which is satisfying. I feel a sense of belonging, a warm, cosy feeling. Now I can join in the others' conversations about spirituality and art – and I enjoy them, too, despite it feeling like a game whose rules I've only just understood. When I want to disagree – and that still happens – I push my critical thoughts aside and say nothing. I throw myself into my weaving projects, which in practice means that I draw and paint fabric designs, imagining that they are colourful architectural plans. I keep putting off working with the loom. The others are full of admiration for my designs, but I can't enjoy their praise because all my work feels slightly meaningless.

~

Ilm Park is getting greener by the day, and my complicated dance with Jakob continues. There are times when we see each other almost regularly. We spend evenings together, sleep with and, now that the weather has turned warm, next to each other, or we stay up talking and drinking for hours. I enjoy the rush I get when I see him, which cords up my throat and makes my ears buzz. Then there are weeks when I barely catch a glimpse of him, and he doesn't show up for our dates. The abrupt switches, between intimacy and stand-offishness, are dizzying. Then I miss him and wonder what he's doing and who he's seeing. I try to remember the calm and reassurance I felt during the semester break, but it is starting to fade more and more. As always, Jakob holds back when others are around, and that bothers me too. Only Samuel knows what's going on, and his interest in my affair is so unrelenting that I sometimes wonder whether he's in love with Jakob himself. I have the feeling that Sidonie suspects something, but she would certainly never bring it up. Her sporadic friendliness towards me has thinned out. Now she makes remarks about 'having to resist the needs of the flesh' while looking at me as if I were an enormous, disgusting beetle, which I obligingly become. I watch Jakob and Johannes together very carefully. With an almost forensic interest, I follow their every move and gesture, never discovering any definite proof. I keep putting off asking Jakob about the matter, and in the end, I decide that Maria's story was simply a rumour.

The first hot days of summer arrive. We're sitting on the roof terrace of the House of the Templars. Erich has chosen this spot for us to sunbathe, and I'm soaking up the heat from the warm tiles. Sidonie is laughing as she tells us about her very first lesson with Johannes, which Jakob missed.

'He put a lemon on the table, and we were asked to depict its essence. I don't think any one of us got it right.'

'But you were the prodigy of the preliminary course,' says Jakob, and the way he smiles at her makes me feel uncomfortable. 'I'm sure you didn't do it wrong!'

'Oh, I did! This is what happened: we all showed him our drawings. Erich had done some wild abstract pictures, Samuel a soft, almost runny lemon, and I had tried to capture the yellow with coloured pens. But Johannes held up the lemon, bit into it and made an awful face. "*That* is the essence of a lemon, that's what you should have shown," he said.' Erich and Samuel join in the laughter. 'You should have seen our faces!'

Jakob and Sidonie outdo each other in praise of Johannes' teaching genius. I can't join in the discussion and feel left out. Our conversations always revolve around our closed little world. I think I'm the only one who reads the newspaper regularly. Last weekend, Walther Rathenau was assassinated by right-wing activists; the whole country is talking about a possible civil war. And what are we doing? We're talking about runny lemons and our diets.

Now Sidonie has started on her favourite topic. The Dutch artist Theo van Doesburg has moved to Weimar and is giving private lessons in his studio, attended by many Bauhaus students.

'He's hoping Gropius will appoint him as a master,' says Jakob.

'Have you seen the terrible drawings by the Doesburg admirer, Peter Röhl?' Sidonie asks but doesn't wait for an answer. 'He drew a caricature of Johannes. He calls him the Thistle Visionary. I don't find that funny at all. Doesburg stirs up resentment towards us in his classes.'

'He should focus on his teaching,' says Samuel.

'If he wants to reduce everything to numbers, including intuition, then there's not much left to teach,' Sidonie replies.

We only notice the two fat constables in front of the House of the Templars when one of them shouts: 'I don't believe it! Those layabouts are sitting on the roof again!'

The older of the two yells: 'Hey, you lot! Come down here at once!'

Erich springs to attention, which, in his lying position and bare chest, looks very funny. 'Of course, Officer! Straight away!'

The rest of us can hardly contain our laughter.

'Ladies and gentlemen, I have no idea what you find so funny, come down here at once, this instant!' The older policeman is all worked up. He waves his arms about, and his face, with its handlebar moustache, goes bright red.

'That's the steward. He's been here before. Come on, I don't want to get into trouble,' says Erich. For his sake, we clamber down the narrow ladder, giggling. At the bottom, Erich tries to placate the two men. We watch the negotiations for a while; then I say I have to get back to the workshop.

Jakob asks if he can come with me and, to my surprise, neither Samuel nor Sidonie decide to join us.

We make a detour through the park. For a while, we say nothing, strolling next to each other, until I eventually say: 'Don't get me wrong, I think Johannes is a wonderful teacher, but I sometimes find there's something strange about your admiration for him.'

'What do you mean?'

'It's so ... unconditional. As if Johannes could do no wrong. But shouldn't everyone be challenged now and again?' I ask.

Jakob stops. 'Why? What's Johannes done?'

'Nothing at all. Nothing bad. Not that I know of, at least. But you all act as if Johannes were a god or some guru who can't be held accountable for anything.'

'I don't understand what you've got against him all of a sudden. And anyway, he's withdrawing from the Bauhaus more and more since Gropius took charge of the workshops,' says Jakob.

'But that's not the point!' I take a deep breath. 'If he makes the rules and you all follow him blindly, what's the difference between you and the philistines who are constantly praying in church? What makes you better than Erich's parents who have rejected their son just because he wanted to study here?'

Jakob shakes his head and looks at me in annoyance. 'I think you're exaggerating.'

'Maybe. But at least I wonder about these things. You never think about anything outside your world. Shouldn't art be political, especially in times like these?'

'But why? If we wanted to be politicians, we wouldn't be here.'

'I'm not talking about the kind of politics that go on in the town hall. It's all getting more extreme, people are beating each other to a pulp, and we're just obsessing about ourselves.'

'Luise, I don't know why we're arguing. It's such nice weather. Can't we just go for a walk?'

I give up. We take the path to the workshops in silence while I carry on the discussion in my head, with all my sound arguments. At the door to the weaving workshop, Jakob says: 'I have to get on with my sculpture now,' and disappears after giving me a brief peck on the cheek. I watch after him for a while, then pull myself together and enter the workshop.

~

Despite the gorgeous weather outside, nearly all the looms are occupied. Whirring and clacking fill the room, a scene of industriousness and productivity, which already grates on my nerves. Like in the main building, large windows look on to the workspaces, and the sun is beating through the glass. The air is dusty. Master Muche is sitting at a loom in the front row with Maria next to him. She hasn't noticed me, and I hesitate before I take a seat at an empty place behind her.

I thread the weft clumsily, probably because of my half-hearted feelings about weaving. There's no great mystery to it. First, you thread the weft; then you shunt the shuttle through the warp, reach the other side and start all over again, till kingdom come. I can stand the monotony of the work, but the looms aren't benevolent leaders. One serves them submissively, and they still make your life difficult. Sometimes the warp snaps or the pedal jams, and if you fasten the yarn wrong even once, you have to thread it up all over again.

Still, I can at least indulge my angry feelings while doing this repetitive work. I don't understand why Sidonie is so eager to be in this workshop: it epitomises the rationalisation and technology that she so stridently condemns all the time. But Sidonie does whatever Johannes tells her to. So much for his teaching genius. Perhaps he was right to say I'm not cut out for the carpentry workshop, but banishing wild Sidonie to study here can't be right.

My weft yarn runs out. The fabric I've started weaving is too loose and looks shoddy. Instead of fetching a new spool, I put down the shuttle and stare at the back of Maria's head through my loom. She is talking quietly to Master Muche. Slight envy comes over me, a longing almost. I'm envious of Maria for being so sure of who she is and where she belongs, that she has a teacher she clearly agrees with and is at peace with her idea of the world and her friends.

Maybe Maria senses my gaze; in any case, she turns around, and her eyes widen. 'Luise! What are you doing here?'

Somehow Maria and I have not run into each other once this semester. I was sure that she knew I'd been consigned to the weaving workshop, but she looks at me in surprise. Since my emotional outburst in her room, I've been avoiding her, not wanting to admit to her that I've lapsed back into my affair with Jakob. And Maria has made no effort to come and see me. I guess she must have at least noticed that I haven't broken off from my friends. I don't want to upset her, but I feel desperate and incapable of holding a conversation with someone who feels so familiar and so alien at the same time. 'I'm in this workshop too now. But I was just on my way out,' is all I manage to say. I hastily clear my place and shout 'See you soon!' in her direction, before walking briskly out of the room.

~

The Bauhaus garden is flourishing. It was planted just two years ago on a slope on the other side of Ilm Park, flanked by a copse of chestnut trees on one side and an army barracks on the other. It mostly grows potatoes but also onions, beetroot and rhubarb for our canteen. My physical stamina has greatly improved due to our regular hikes, but I am still out of breath at the last few yards. I stop and look around for Jakob. I spot Sidonie, whose red curls are visible behind a raspberry bush. As I get nearer, I see Samuel and Jakob who are kneeling on the ground and weeding.

Samuel looks up at me, his smeared glasses aslant on his nose, and says: 'Ah, Luise, are you here to help with the weeding?'

'I'm here to meet Jakob,' I say.

Sidonie throws Jakob a probing look before he says hurriedly, 'Luise and I wanted to talk about a project that we might do together.' He brushes the dirt off his trousers, and we say goodbye. Some parts of the slope have been left fallow; this is the site of the future Bauhaus student residencies.

As soon as we're out of sight, I say, 'So, we're doing a project together, that's interesting.' From his expression, it's obvious he'd hoped I would overlook his excuse. Instead of replying, he takes my hand and pulls me toward him. With blistering coldness I ask, 'What kind of project is it exactly?'

He lets go of my hand again, like someone giving up. 'Listen, Luise. Things are good the way they are. If we tell everyone about us, they'll only get involved. It would put pressure on us, and there's no need for that.'

'What would we tell them about us anyway? I don't know what "us" is!'

'But why do we have to define it? Look at all those conventional marriages. Do you think that relationships get better when they're defined and restricted?'

Now he's got me. If I argue with him, I'm conventional and unimaginative; if I don't, I legitimise his slippery ways. We walk in silence across the grounds, which are dense with clover and bordered by a few villas to our right. To distract myself, I try to picture how the plot of land could be developed into student and teacher accommodation; not an easy task as the chestnut trees should stay. Perhaps scattering the buildings among the trees would be nice.

Jakob says: 'Have you heard of the Aryana House?' I shake my head stubbornly, but he's undeterred. 'It's in Switzerland, in a place called Herrliberg. It's a house where only Mazdaznan followers live. They have a printing press and a bakery. They even produce soap suited to different temperaments. It's right on Lake Zurich, in the middle of the countryside. It sounds wonderful, don't you think?' I'm still not ready to give up my resistance. Then he adds: 'I'm thinking about going there for a week before the holidays. I'd be back in time for the kite festival, and I'm sure we could persuade the masters that it's part of our training. Come with me!' I look at him incredulously.

A whole week together, without these periods of estrangement that are starting to seem increasingly unnatural? 'Ok, then. If you like,' I say, giving myself away with a delighted smile.

~

There are still three whole days before we're due to leave. Nevertheless, I prepare my clothes, sort out books and debate which suitcase I should take. In the end, I decide on the smaller one. Since I've been wearing my monk's jacket, I only ever change between two pairs of trousers: I haven't worn my clothes from Berlin in months. Just to be prepared, I pack the make-up bag Charlotte gave me, although I doubt I'll have the opportunity to use it in Herrliberg. Since our first excursions, I have realised that I don't like being in nature. Although the views from the top of Ettersberg mountain or the Horn on to Ilm valley are very nice, they don't outweigh the strain of hiking uphill. Nature has always seemed hostile to me, and I can't understand why anyone would willingly give up the comforts of civilisation. But I keep this thought to myself. Whenever Sidonie talks about the cleansing powers of nature, I nod in agreement.

There's a knock at my bedroom door. Jakob sticks his head around the door. Frau Werner is strangely laissez-faire about my gentleman visitor. I hope she doesn't know that he sometimes spends the night here, but she fell for Jakob's boyish charm the first time he came on an official visit for afternoon coffee and cake.

'A letter just arrived,' says Jakob with a strained smile. 'My mother has fallen ill and I have to return to Austria straight away.'

I don't know what I was expecting. Of course we can't just go away together. Of course something had to come up. I squash my disappointment because I know how much Jakob loves his mother and try my best to seem understanding and sympathetic. He doesn't know the details yet. The letter is from his mother's neighbour, and he couldn't glean much from it except her concern for his mother, and that he should come home as soon as possible. Jakob is visibly relieved that I don't start a fight or make a scene, and he looks at me with a distracted tenderness.

'You can go to Switzerland on your own,' he says. 'Perhaps one of the others will want to go with you – Erich or Samuel, for example.' He doesn't understand that the house in Herrliberg itself doesn't interest me at all, and that I only agreed to go to spend a whole week without missing him.

And now he's going away without me and can't even say when he'll be back.

~

Over the next few days, I find it harder than usual to concentrate in the workshop. I can't seem to finish weaving my fabric and the other students are already moaning because I'm always hogging the loom. Instead of working on my design, I go to the station and check the timetable to see which train Jakob might have taken. Then I buy myself a map of Austria and check the exact location of Auersthal, his home village. But I still don't feel any closer to him. After a week, I can't bear it any more and think about sending a telegram. Samuel probably has his address. A telegram seems to suggest urgency, but I don't have anything to say. Maybe a letter? But what if it arrives after Jakob leaves Auersthal? In the end, I write the most harmless note possible on my headed notepaper under the pretext that Georg Muche wants to know when Jakob might be back. When I send it off, I feel a little better; then my nervousness returns twice as strong.

On the evening of the kite festival, I walk over to the House of the Templars to meet the others. We only want to show our faces at the festival before leaving. It's warm, but so windy this time that Gropius seems to have sealed a pact with the weather god to make kite-flying possible. Thinking about last year's party makes me wistful. I think of my four-headed hydra, Maria and my excitement. Everything had seemed possible back then: a love affair with Jakob, a career as an architect or a group of friends with whom I could feel entirely at home.

The wind tugs at the big wooden door. When I finally manage to open it and go in, the only thing I see is Sidonie's red head of hair. She's standing by a small table in the corner, preparing her revolting tea. Without turning around, she says, 'Erich and Samuel have already gone for an evening walk. Would you like a cup of hot root juice?' Because I still want Sidonie to like me, I say yes, and try not to make a face at the first sip. We don't say anything. She doesn't seem to mind the silence, while it makes me nervous. I try hard to think of things to fill it. Johannes is neutral ground, and besides, she always likes talking about him. I ask her if he's going to be at the kite festival.

'Johannes has been in Herrliberg for the past week,' says Sidonie, obviously surprised that I haven't noticed his absence. An uneasy feeling creeps over me. Is that why Jakob wanted to go there? But then why take me?

'In Switzerland?' I ask.

'Yes, I wish I could have gone. I heard that they make everything themselves there, and the vegetables are planted in a big garden. They meditate and go on hikes together. It's probably much easier to follow our rules when you live in a big Mazdaznan community. Jakob could hardly bring himself to leave.'

'Jakob went there too?'

'You didn't know? He came back yesterday.'

Sidonie is genuinely astonished, but there is a glitter of triumph in her green eyes. I feel like I've been pushed off the top of a high tower into a bottomless crater. Then another feeling streams in, an impatient restlessness. It's as if I finally have proof of something that I've always known. The latent untruth of our relationship, which stopped me from completely trusting Jakob, has finally come to light. At least I feel slightly less insane now. Being angry at Jakob is better than constantly doubting myself. I feel the need to confront him straight away.

'Is Jakob coming tonight?' My voice catches. Sidonie merely shrugs and drops to the floor with boyish grace. I sit down next to her, spilling half my tea in the process.

Erich and Samuel come charging through the door. They are red-cheeked and tell us cheerfully about their walk. I am in the grip of my panicked thoughts about Jakob. Perhaps they know where he is, but I don't want to ask in front of Sidonie. At some point, I realise he's not coming. He's probably at the festival already. But Sidonie has just brewed a new pot of root juice, and the three of them become engrossed in conversation.

After an interminable half an hour, I say: 'Shouldn't we be going? The kite-flying is probably over already.'

To my relief, Sidonie says, 'You're right. Everyone's probably at the Ilmschlösschen by now,' and stands up. I curse the long walk through the park on the Ilm, and even secretly curse Erich, who slows us down terribly. I have to exert every ounce of self-control not to snap at him. Once we arrive at the Ilmschlösschen, I part from the others and start looking for Jakob. I hate the curious glances that people throw each other when you do the rounds at a party alone. It's crowded and hot, and large kites keep blocking my way.

There he is. I forget how handsome he is every time. With a freshly starched shirt and shiny curls, he's standing in a corner and talking to a girl I've never seen before. When he sees me, he cheerily waves me over. My palms are clammy, but my rage gives me an icy clarity. I ignore the girl, who tries to greet me, and say: 'Let's go outside – it's loud in here.' Jakob first throws me an inquisitive look, then looks at the girl apologetically and follows me outside.

Without looking back, I go down the street, away from the Ilmschlösschen. 'Luise, where are you going?' Jakob asks behind me.

I walk faster. Finally, we reach the park. Then I stop and say: 'You make up a story about your mother being ill, just so that you can spend time with Johannes in the mountains. That's low, even by your standards, Jakob. But what I still don't get is why you invited me in the first place? It just made everything more complicated for you.'

The surprise on Jakob's face remains, but his demeanour instantly switches from being friendly to hurt. 'But my mother *was* ill! It just wasn't as serious as I thought. And when the telegram from Johannes came, I thought that I might as well spend the rest of the time in Switzerland. That wasn't a deceitful plan. You're completely insane.' His expression reveals something else now – contempt, maybe.

'But why didn't you think about writing *me* a telegram?'

'I thought you didn't want to go. You could have gone by yourself.'

Now, besides feeling anger, I feel inconsolable. I don't want some lukewarm, erratic love affair.

'I don't want this,' I say, and all the energy drains from my body. I feel very, very tired.

'But Luise, there were no bad intentions on my part. I didn't realise that you were so keen on going to Herrliberg.'

'Just admit it: you didn't want me there. You wanted to spend time with Johannes on your own.'

'What are you trying to say?'

'You may not know this, but the entire school is talking about you two behind your backs. Only I was fool enough to trust you.'

'What on earth is that supposed to mean? Johannes is my mentor, that's it.'

And so we continue, round and round in circles, following a choreography of anger, exasperation, placation and frustration. Every time I think I've finally destroyed the bond between us and set myself free, Jakob succeeds in pulling me back in. Then he says something that angers me all over again, and we start the next round.

Eventually, we are both simply too exhausted to continue. It is late at night, and I wonder how we have managed to spend so many hours in dark intoxication on this hill. Side by side, we silently trudge down through the park. When we reach my house, we kiss. It is the last, desperate attempt at salvation. Like so many times before, we tiptoe into my room, but this time, the sex is different: we cling to each other, we fight, we draw it out, because we both sense that it is the last time. We come together. My orgasm dampens my sadness for a second; then I start crying. Stubbornly, I twist myself out of Jakob's arms because I have to do my routine of douching, a habit that I have finally got used to, but which feels completely out of place right now. When I return, Jakob is asleep. This time, my head is empty and my body exhausted enough to fall asleep too.

The next morning, I wake up alone.

~

The fasting period begins again, but I don't feel the same euphoria as last time, even after the first few days. In a dull trance, I go on hikes in the autumn drizzle. Getting up at dawn has sapped me of all my energy and I drag myself to the weaving workshop and back to my room at Frau Werner's. I avoid the House of the Templars. One grey day merges into the next. After five days, for the first time, I secretly think about eating something. No one would notice, and no one would know if I slept in either. And at the moment, sleep is the only escape from the pain, from constantly thinking about Jakob, from thoughts that steadily take on a life of their own, a merry-go-round of self-doubt, memories and blame. Every morning I make a new deal with myself, and each time I give myself a few more minutes' sleep.

Sidonie is the only one of my friends whom I regularly see in the weaving workshop. She tells me they are planning to visit Johannes just after dawn on his birthday and sing a song outside his door. Although I have no desire to see Jakob, and Johannes is the last person I want to please, I miss doing things with my friends and decide to join them.

No negotiations with myself today; I get up at five o'clock sharp, slip on my robes and plod off sleepily towards Frauenplan. That's where we've arranged to meet and surprise Johannes. Samuel and Erich are pleased to see me: they hug me and scold me for not having shown my face in such a long time. Their attention does me good. I look around guardedly, but Jakob isn't there. I feel relieved and disappointed at the same time. A few people have brought homemade gifts, and someone has decorated a long branch which is now swinging festively in the air. It's a cold November day and dawn gingerly lights up the streets. I shiver and wish I was back in my warm bed. The others don't seem to be suffering as much from our self-imposed regime of sleep and food deprivation. There is subdued but lively laughter and chatter. Only Erich looks unwell, his dark complexion has gone ashen grey. As for Samuel, I wonder how his lanky body can bear our regimens. But although he's always imagining illnesses, he doesn't look as if he's suffering at all, quite the contrary in fact. And, as usual when we're out as a group, his shyness disappears almost straight away.

Finally, we're all assembled and set off in convoy. The murmurs, which we've kept respectfully low, get louder and one group even starts singing. When we reach Johannes' house, everyone has joined in. 'Itten, Muche, Mazdaznan! Maz-daz-nan, Maz-daz-nan' is our simplistic tune. For about ten minutes, nothing happens. We fall silent, and some even wonder out loud if we should leave. But at last the door opens and Johannes steps outside. He's wearing a dressing gown and looks sleepy.

I stare around at the others, outraged, but they are already singing 'Happy Birthday'. Then Johannes gives a brief speech about the importance of the community, solidarity and love. I'm flabbergasted that our master – our mentor, as some call him – clearly does not practise what he preaches. It's completely obvious that he does not get up at dawn. Who knows whether or not he fasts? I can't believe that I'm the only one who finds his hypocrisy offensive. I look around again, but all I see on the faces around me is respect and admiration. Johannes asks us in and makes tea in large pots.

I sit silently with the others in the living room, not touching my tea. When the group finally starts to break up, I quickly say goodbye and am glad to walk back alone. At home, I throw my cloak in a corner and go straight to the pantry. Inside there is a large, glistening ham that a friendly farmer gave Frau Werner. Standing over it, I take a knife, and without a plate, cut off juicy slices of meat and stuff them into my mouth. Contented and full, I go back to bed and sleep for the rest of the day.

~

Over the next few weeks, I sleep and eat a lot and resume my attempts to learn something in the carpentry workshop. So far, no one has noticed that I'm attending the weaving workshop ever more rarely – perhaps because it's the biggest workshop on campus. Helene Börner, the master of works for weaving under Muche, keeps a close eye on things, but it seems that not even she can stay completely on top of it all.

Some of the carpentry students know me from when I was working on my sculpture in the preliminary course. Gropius has taken over since then, but he hardly ever turns up, so I never need to explain myself. The other students don't ask any questions either. I'm in a kind of limbo because all the others seem to be working on joint projects, while I just fiddle around without any guidance. Still, it gives me the chance to get to know the tools and learn some of the basics. In the end, though, without a bigger goal, what I'm doing feels meaningless.

One day, I'm using the large saw when someone taps me on the shoulder. It's the ginger boy who ignored my suggestions for the Sommerfeld House last time. 'What are you working on?' he asks.

Startled, I step back from the machine, not knowing what to say. If I'm found out, I'll probably end up back in the weaving workshop. As confidently as possible, I say, 'Oh, nothing special. An independent piece of work.'

'But we're supposed to be working on the exhibition,' the boy objects. I know, of course, what he's talking about. A major Bauhaus exhibition is being organised for next summer to convince the citizens of Weimar and the state that the work we're doing here is worthwhile. The whole school is working on it.

I shrug and turn my attention back to the wood. But the boy won't let up. 'When did you join the carpentry workshop anyway?'

There's no point: he's not going to leave me in peace. Impulsively, I grab his sleeve and pull him over to the door. 'Listen,' I say, 'officially, I'm not even a student here. It's just that I hate the weaving workshop.'

To my complete astonishment, the boy starts laughing. And he doesn't stop. He has a throaty chuckle that makes him sound slightly insane. I stare at him, nonplussed. He finally manages to pull himself together, wipes the tears from his eyes and says: 'Ah, a rebel! Excellent. My name's Friedrich, by the way.'

'Luise,' I say and shake his outstretched hand. I don't quite trust our truce, but his face expresses only admiration or mirth, definitely not animosity.

Blinking and brushing some wood shavings from his red hair, he asks if I want to have a bite to eat with him after we've finished our work. A few hours later, we're sitting in the canteen. The likelihood of bumping into my friends here is slim because they're fasting. But I can't shake the feeling that I'm doing something forbidden, sitting here in front of a plate of steaming lentils. I'm so nervous that I can barely concentrate on what Friedrich is saying. He has an angular face and talks very fast. He often sounds like he's making grave statements, and when he talks, his small, deep-set eyes blink very quickly.

I slowly forget that no one is supposed to see me here. Friedrich doesn't ask any questions about what I'm doing, and it's fun to listen to him. He talks about Mussolini, gets worked up and explains with an urgency I'm not used to that Germany has to stop things from going the same way as in Italy.

'But that's not very likely anyway under the Social Democrats,' I say.

Friedrich laughs scornfully. 'No, we can't rely on the Social Democrats to fight fascism.'

Friedrich is a communist. I find that fascinating. I've never met anyone with such clear-cut political views. But how could I when my friends hardly show any interest in politics? Not only that but the Council of Masters has recently prohibited any political associations at the Bauhaus. Friedrich takes no notice of this: he has an opinion on everything. He complains that the art we make here is not proletarian enough.

At last I see the chance to pour my heart out to someone. Hesitantly and vaguely, I try to explain my thoughts to him.

I tell him that I don't find it very radical to cling to the radical ideas of the previous decade, but that whenever I start talking about craftsmanship and technology, people look at me doubtfully. It's not that I want to return to the days of the Grand Ducal Art School, the forerunner to the Bauhaus: I want to try out something new, something different that hasn't already been done by our teachers. But no matter how hard I try to make my friends understand, my criticism bounces off them, and they think that I'm stuck in the past.

Friedrich immediately understands what I'm talking about. He says that Itten's acolytes don't know a thing about architecture and they regard buildings as accommodation for people, not expressions of social structures. He talks about the hegemony of the bourgeoisie, about the means of production and improved conditions for workers. I wonder what all this has to do with architecture, but I don't say so. I feel agitated and tired at the same time, and my energy is slowly fading. The canteen has long since emptied. By the time we finally step out into the cold winter air, even Friedrich has fallen silent.

~

I lay into the Christmas roast with a huge appetite, and my mother is relieved that I have got over 'that vegetarian nonsense'. She had been worried. True, I have lost weight: my bony hips seem wider, and my breasts regrettably small. But how is my mother supposed to know that the main reason for the nauseous feeling in my stomach is my break-up with Jakob. I saw him twice again before the holidays, both times from a distance. We didn't talk. It feels good to be back in the big city again, even though the silent evening meals and my father's sternness weigh me down me a little more every year. Otto is here too this time, and as soon as my father isn't around, he orders my mother and me about. In the past, I used to do what he said without question. But this time, I talk back to him. Otto ignores me and Mother undermines my protest by saying, 'Don't argue now, children,' then fetches whatever he wants. I feel annoyed at my mother, but above all, I envy Otto's ability to assert himself. At mealtimes, he talks about politics until my father and mother forbid him to do so. But that only happens when Otto has got sufficiently worked up to make one of his little speeches. He thrashes about with his great big hands, talks about Bavarian rights, Jewish money and the Germany People's Party, to which several of his friends belong. After my father has managed to silence him one way or another, the only sound is his demonstrative chomping.

After our Christmas dinner, my father summons me for a talk. We withdraw to his study. I feel important and adult because this room is normally reserved for discussions with business partners and clients. As a child, I wasn't even allowed to come in here. The dark wood panelling expresses the same unhurried gravity that I know so well from my father. Nothing is just lying around. The plans and construction drawings that I would like to look at are neatly filed away in opaque folders. Unlike the rest of our rooms, his study is quite chilly, as if he wants to demonstrate that my mother's warm-heartedness cannot permeate all areas of the house. This room is governed by the Prussian spirit so dear to my father, but which I find increasingly alien.

I don't have to wonder for long what he wants to discuss with me. He gets straight to the point. 'So, Luise, explain to me what exactly it is you're learning at that college.'

I know there is little point in explaining the preliminary course to my father, so I get to the weaving workshop. I go into detail, talking about warp rollers and back beams, using as many technical terms as I can. With a gesture that feels familiar to me, he indicates that I should be quiet. I obey. He seems to be thinking. Finally, he says abruptly, 'Good, that will be all.' He picks up a folder from the desk and flips it open. I try to scrutinise which project it might be; but, with a curt look, he signals that it is time I left his domain.

The very next morning, my mother takes me aside. I don't immediately get what she's trying to say to me, because she brings such discretion to questions that are indiscreet by nature. When I realise that she wants to know whether I have admirers and whether there is a potential husband among these admirers, I suddenly think of Jakob and feel sick. So that's why the conversation with my father was so short yesterday. They have obviously divided up the task of interrogating me. I have never talked to my mother about such things. It's out of the question to tell her about Jakob. I beat around the bush for ages until I have managed to deny the existence of any admirers. My mother looks at me with concern but doesn't ask any further questions. Perhaps she is as relieved as I am that the conversation is finally over.

I keep my distance from Charlotte and our Berlin friends because I can't bear the thought of extravagant parties and loud music. Charlotte's cheerful chatter, her ease with strangers and her coquetry grate on me. It is as though she were the female incarnation of Jakob; characteristics I had only recently thought of as brilliant virtues and now associate with shallowness and superficiality. For hours on end, I sit in my room mulling things over, as if this is the only way I can find out what went on between Jakob and Johannes, why things didn't work out between Jakob and me, and why he doesn't love me enough. My mother's Christmas present – a pair of fine leather shoes with delicate heels and decorative design – is very beautiful, but they rub my feet. I promise myself that by the time I've worn them in, it will no longer hurt to think of Jakob.

On New Year's Eve, I sit with my parents, who have invited some friends, a married couple. Otto is away on business, and the guests leave shortly after midnight. It is quiet. Soon afterwards, I'm lying in bed, unable to sleep. For a long time, I stare at the soft silhouettes of the furniture in my room and think back on the past year. I want to linger in this cocoon of maternal love and inertia for a while longer. But the inevitable January morning, when I eventually take the train back to Weimar, arrives sooner than I would like.

~

I am just about to unpack my clothes and put them away in my drawer when the doorbell rings. Friedrich comes charging up the stairs and starts chattering immediately. I think his lack of tact has to do with the fact that he is constantly preoccupied with theories, analyses and utopias. Superficial things like manners are probably unimportant to him. He certainly doesn't notice that all my clothes, including my underwear, are lying about the room. Nor does he ask how long I've been back or how my Christmas holiday was. He simply sits down on my bed and carries on talking.

' ... which doesn't surprise me. French imperialism, of course, has the military power to do it. But they shouldn't count on not provoking a war that way.' I try to concentrate on what he's saying.

'War? What are you talking about?'

'Luise, where have you been for the past few days? The French and the Belgians have occupied the Ruhr. The government has ordered a general strike and called for passive resistance.' Well, I have heard this news, of course. I just hadn't expected that the subject would be raised quite so quickly or in my bedroom. And besides, it wouldn't have occurred to me to think of war again so soon.

'Do you think there's going to be another war?' I ask Friedrich.

'Well, this so-called government certainly isn't just going to hand over the Ruhr. The petite bourgeoisie and swastika folk with their nationalist slogans think they can use the Ruhr workers to impose their interests. And the German Communist Party wants to demonstrate national reliability and supports the strike. A party truce doesn't benefit anyone.'

'But the Communist Party supported the strike two years ago.'

'Yes, but that was different. Now it's joining the capitalists' side,' says Friedrich, staring grimly into the distance and blinking a few times. Then he says, 'I know you can keep a secret.' I don't realise at first that he's asking me a question, but then he looks up at me expectantly. So I nod vigorously.

'Of course!'

He says: 'A few comrades told me that there are plans to assist the government actively.' Friedrich sees that I don't understand, so he adds: 'Let's just say, in an explosive way . . . ' I hate it when people use weighty allusions instead of just saying something straight out, but at least I get what he's talking about now.

'Bombs? Are you trying to stop a war or instigate one?' I'm too loud for Friedrich, who raises his hand and looks around, terrified.

'Listen, I'm against it! The proletariat has no Fatherland, the fight for one nation is just a distraction. Not that I have anything against drastic means, but if it bolsters the reaction . . . Anyway, I'm only telling you what I heard.'

After I've finally got rid of Friedrich, and have unpacked and stowed away my clothes, I start to wonder where he gets his information. I read the newspapers too, of course, but who is telling him this kind of thing in Weimar? I'm sure such sensitive information can't be sent by telegraph. It's impressive to think that there is a network spreading information this fast by word of mouth. I have always thought of Friedrich as a loner, but there must be people at the Bauhaus who think the way he does.

~

The small studio on Schanzengraben is packed. Friedrich has dragged me along to a lecture by Theo van Doesburg. Although I've avoided seeing Sidonie and the others until now, it feels like a betrayal. But I'm curious too. Students sit everywhere, some on chairs, some on the floor, or even on the two work benches that have been moved into the corner. Van Doesburg is a tall man with a high forehead, his hairline hidden beneath an American cap. While the room is still filling up, he starts his lecture. He talks about his last two years in Weimar, and I realise that this is his farewell speech. That doesn't stop him declaring his principles one last time. In a lively but routine manner, he talks about a new industrial style, which can only come about by using machines 'in the right way'. Craftsmanship is no longer sufficient. It's outdated, he says, and has been outrun by technical developments. He becomes agitated as he talks, complaining about the 'romantic fuzzy thinking' that still holds sway at the Bauhaus and the 'die-hards' who resist technical progress at all cost. He seems vain to me, standing there in his sports gear, but I'm also fascinated by how different his worldview is.

Does the rest of the Bauhaus see it the same way? Does the worker's fear of automation mean anything to them? I steal a glance at Friedrich, who is listening raptly. Does he think I'm outdated?

Van Doesburg ends his speech with an appeal to uphold the principles of constructivism after he leaves. He speaks warmly of the KURI group – which I've never heard of before – then bids a final grand farewell. Resounding applause follows and people chant: 'Van Doesburg should stay!' and 'Van Doesburg for director!' Then, amid cheering and interjections, a slim student recites a farewell poem that seems totally devoid of meaning. A convoluted, colourful sculpture is dragged on to the stage; van Doesburg accepts his leaving present with an exceedingly humble bow. Attention wanes, wine is served, and a babble of voices rises.

Friedrich is being hogged by two people to whom he doesn't introduce me. He even turns his back on me. Minutes go by while I wonder whether Friedrich is just socially awkward, or whether he's embarrassed by me. Although I'm not in my monk's jacket, the university is so small that I'm probably known as someone from Itten's circle. When the other two leave, at last, he seems surprised to find me still sitting next to him. I want to go home, and Friedrich immediately says he'll come with me. I reprimand myself for being so paranoid. He's clearly much too caught up in his world for me to embarrass him.

On our way through the dimly lit streets, Friedrich tells me about the Dada-Constructivist Congress that van Doesburg organised last summer. 'He's incredibly vain, you're right, but not all of what he says is stupid. The artists he persuaded to visit Weimar for the congress are all trying out new methods. I went to Berlin quite often last year and looked at all kinds of things; I went to every exhibition opening. There was a lot of crap going on. But the people van Doesburg invited were the ones who had something to say.'

'And what's KURI?' I ask.

Friedrich rolls his eyes. 'A group of people from Bauhaus who try to put everything that van Doesburg says into practice. But you know that I don't fall for group hype. Apart from that, they're completely unpolitical – and in times like these! They're even against the appointment of Hungarian artist Moholy-Nagy. There are rumours that he will be taken on as a master. I went to his exhibition in Berlin – good stuff. But van Doesburg has been making a fuss about him because he says he's too political. I think it would be great to finally have a socialist teach here.'

My head is spinning. The evening's impressions coat the familiar, slightly worn Mazdaznan worldview. Jakob and the others seem very far away all of a sudden.

~

I avoid the weaving workshop over the next few weeks, but Johannes is giving a lecture in the House of the Templars; I want to give it another chance and I can't dodge my friends for much longer. Besides, I miss Samuel and Erich. I put on my monk's jacket, which feels like a costume again, and trudge through the cold air. It hasn't snowed yet this winter, but it's windy and damp. I know the way so well that it almost makes me aggressive. Another disadvantage to small-town life: there are never any new buildings, bars or even new posters to discover.

Besides Johannes and Sidonie, who is almost never on time, everyone is already there when I push open the heavy door to the fireplace room. Jakob is standing in the corner talking to a girl I don't know. The pair of them look sweet and carefree, standing there chatting, he in his usual collar-less shirt, she in a spotless white dress. It makes me furious and jealous. I try not to look over in their direction. I leave out that whole corner to be on the safe side. Luckily, Erich and Samuel are standing at the other end of the room, and I walk straight over to them.

'Where have you been all this time?' Samuel asks in greeting, with an accusatory tone in his voice. I shrug and distract him by bombarding them with questions about their health. Erich has got even thinner, and despite his dark complexion, he looks pale and hollow-cheeked. His voice, which always dragged a little, sounds weak. But he insists he is in fine health. Samuel, on the other hand, complains about his various ailments. I cautiously look in Jakob's direction; he doesn't even seem to have noticed me. Samuel gets it right away. 'That's Frida Gerber over there in the white dress. Johannes brought her back from Herrliberg.'

'Brought her back? As a souvenir?' I say, immediately regretting my sarcasm. Erich and Samuel exchange looks and change the subject.

Sidonie joins us and immediately makes herself the centre of attention. She wants to talk about Frida too, and is not restrained by tact. 'I heard that she was brought up according to the Mazdaznan teachings by her parents. And you can tell straight away! She's so poised, and she makes it look so effortless. Compared to her, we're absolute beginners.'

Samuel nods enthusiastically. 'I talked to her earlier for a moment. She's open and friendly, but at the same time, she has this mysterious air. I wish I had her grace.'

Even Erich, who is not one for going into raptures, has something to add: 'I heard that she had a personal reception with Hanish on his first European tour.'

The three of them can't stop themselves. They outdo each other in their praise for the girl. My jealousy destroys my self-preservation instincts. I listen, captivated, even asking questions. The only thing I don't ask about is her relation to Jakob; for that, my imagination is perfectly sufficient. In my mind, I see the pair of them going for long autumn walks when Jakob was there in secret, by the lake in Herrliberg, or sitting together at the evening meetings.

The extent of his betrayal, which I'm now well aware of, shakes me to the core; I feel angry and humiliated but also disappointed. I feel that I've betrayed myself. Apparently, I've been clinging to a final shred of hope, and I'm not as indifferent to him as I'd like to be. How stupid of me to have thrown accusations at Jakob because of Johannes, when his interests lie elsewhere. I don't know whether or not to be relieved when the conversation takes another turn, namely to Johannes' future at the Bauhaus and his fights with Gropius.

Sidonie acts like she's in the know. 'Johannes hasn't felt comfortable here for a long time. He says he feels like we have withdrawn to a romantic island,' she says.

'No wonder, considering how Gropius has treated him. First, he gave Johannes all the responsibility and work, then he wasn't satisfied with his teaching all of a sudden and took it away from him again,' says Samuel.

Sidonie nods. 'Some students hadn't even finished the projects that Johannes was supervising. But perhaps it's a good thing, to stay out of it and not teach any more. These technology fetishists! You only have to look at Frida to understand that we can't thrive in this environment.'

I become aware that Sidonie is behaving strangely towards Erich. He has tried several times to say something, but each time she has interrupted him. If he manages to get a word in with his slow way of speaking, she rolls her eyes impatiently. My silence is noticed.

'Luise, what do you think?' Sidonie asks and eyes me sharply.

I think back to my conversations with Friedrich, my aversion to nature, my secret stockpile of food during the fasting period, and all of a sudden, I feel like a complete fraud. I want to get away from these people and their ideas. Sidonie is waiting for my answer. 'I don't feel like I have to distance myself from this environment,' I say. 'I think there's great promise in technological progress, especially for architecture. And quite honestly, I have no idea where your obsession with purity is supposed to lead.'

At last I feel as if I'm saying what I think. But from the others' expressions, I can see what I've always been afraid of: that I don't belong here any more. Samuel looks surprised, Erich a little sad and Sidonie triumphant, as if I have finally confirmed what she always thought about me. I even think I can see her doing a breathing exercise to keep herself free of my negative energy.

She says quietly to Samuel: 'There's just no helping some people.'

Something like righteous anger swells up in me. Now that I have come this far, I am ready for confrontation. 'That's exactly what I'm talking about, Sidonie. This—'

I'm interrupted by Johannes' arrival. He's standing at the centre of the room, and everyone focuses their attention on him. It goes very quiet. In my present emotional state, it's impossible to listen to him talk about unity and community. As inconspicuously as possible, I try to weave my way towards the exit; I stumble, people give me dirty looks, and I meet Jakob's eye for the first time that evening. At long last, I manage to reach the door, abandon all self-control and let the door clang shut noisily behind me. Breathing heavily, I walk away, further and further from these people and their cult.

~

The next few months drag by. I spend a lot of time with Friedrich in the carpentry workshop. We're working on our plans for the women's room in the model house that will be presented in the summer. Muche, who designed the house, but is still standing in as master of form in the weaving workshop for Johannes, has seen me a couple of times in the carpentry workshop. Perhaps we still have the same agreement as last year; in any case, he hasn't said anything. Unlike Johannes, he's not one for confrontations. It's lucky for me that Johannes has withdrawn from teaching.

Shortly after Christmas, Friedrich puts me in charge of the dressing table, and I work on it like a madwoman, often late into the night. I'm flattered that he trusts me so much – and I want to prove myself. My hard work hasn't gone unnoticed, and my skills are improving. Although I didn't design the dresser, it's satisfying to be building something, to watch it develop, knowing it will be put to use. It is made up of several parts, and two mirrors are going to be added, while the surface will be fitted with opaque glass. The smaller mirror will be held by long, intersected mechanical arms. An oblong cupboard forms one side of the dresser, a small table the other. I am using a lighter wood to make the drawers and frame.

I've almost finished and want to show it to Friedrich

today, to go over the final details. On my way to the carpentry workshop, I spot a group in monk's jackets. When I look a little closer, I see Sidonie, Samuel and Erich among them, as well as Jakob, unsurprisingly hand in hand with Frida. They're probably just setting off on one of their hikes. Seeing them all gathered together, I finally realise that I no longer belong. A bitter taste rises in my throat and my stomach aches. Nothing has been resolved; everything has been left unsaid. I wonder why people talk about scorched earth – that suggests clarity. But social structures are untidy and muddled, the battle lines blurred and the whispering invisible. For a moment, I feel a strong urge to go over and talk to them, as though I could reverse everything if only I were sociable enough. But then my pride asserts itself. I carry on walking.

Friedrich is sitting in front of my dresser. Although I know he's not interested in such matters, I'm still brooding over my lost friends. I can't help thinking aloud. 'I've always doubted myself, but perhaps it has nothing to do with logic. They're always so concerned with the mystery of things, with enigmas. There's no room for logic. It's all just a huge sham.'

Friedrich blinks impatiently. 'Of course. But that's obvious.' He points to the dresser. 'The drawer here at the top doesn't shut properly.'

'And you know what the worst part is? They immediately decide who has negative energy, who is impure and who isn't up to their standards. I don't think they even understand that this exclusivity contradicts their ideas about love and unity.'

Friedrich murmurs something. It's clear that I won't get him interested in the topic. He says: 'I'm not sure whether we should make the drawers in a lighter wood after all. It's just unnecessary decoration.'

I try to concentrate on the dresser. The contrast between dark and light wood is important to me, I think it's beautiful. But I know that's not the way to convince Friedrich. 'The different types of wood do have a function, Friedrich. They show you where the drawers go.'

My explanation seems to make sense to him, and we stick with using different kinds of wood. I have to sand down the drawers, but otherwise, Friedrich is very happy. The dresser is unadorned and well crafted. He won't have any problems passing it off as his own work. He promises to split what little money he gets for it with me. 'And I won't waste a second!' That's his bitter joke about inflation: everyone is suffering at the moment. I've never had to worry about my upkeep, and my only concern is the logistics of receiving the money my parents send me. They can only do it via telegraph these days because it's hardly worth anything when I receive it otherwise. I'm comfortable compared to the others, but I still feel uneasy about what the whole situation means for my family. Friedrich is well-versed in economic matters, because most of the time he's preoccupied with the class struggle.

He must know that my family is on the other side of this battle, but we've never actually talked about it. I know that my parents would never let me know if they had financial problems, certainly not by letter or telegram. So I screw up my courage and ask: 'Do you think I should be worried about my family?'

'Worried in what sense?'

'Well, about money . . . because of inflation.'

Friedrich laughs. 'Luise, the big industrialists in Berlin are rubbing their hands in glee right now because their debts are dwindling to nothing. No, on the contrary, your family is profiting from this hyperinflation,' he says and blinks emphatically.

'How do you know that my father is an industrialist?'

Friedrich laughs at me again. 'There aren't that many Schillings in Berlin. And I see it as my duty to inform myself about people as much as possible.'

I feel embarrassed for asking, but also uncomfortable: Friedrich, and probably his entire obscure network, have known details about my family the whole time, and have never said a word. But perhaps I should be thankful that my family has never been an obstacle to our friendship.

~

I'm alone in the carpentry workshop, still working on the drawers. It's impossible to get them to shut smoothly, no matter how much I sand and polish them. After sanding one side for the fifth time, I give up, annoyed, and stare out of the window at the grey February skies. The fasting period has started again, and I'm very glad not to have to stick to the Mazdaznan rules any more. There's not much tasty food available as it is, but at least I can dig in if the opportunity arises. I wonder whether I should stop and go to the canteen when I hear someone climbing the stairs in a hurry, and a moment later, Samuel bursts through the door.

He's completely out of breath; his glasses almost slip off his nose. 'Luise, you have to come at once! It's Erich . . . he's, he's . . . I don't know what to do.'

I struggle to get him to calm down and sit on a chair in the workshop. 'Slowly. What's the matter with Erich?' I ask.

'He's ill! First, we thought it was just a cold. But then it got worse, and since last night, he's had a very high temperature. He's no longer conscious. I think his leg injury is infected. I'm really worried, Luise.'

'Have you called a doctor?'

'No! Sidonie doesn't trust doctors, and she says we can't afford them anyway. But perhaps you – you have some medicine somewhere?'

To my surprise, Samuel's panic has the effect of making me very lucid and calm. I think hard. 'Frau Werner must still have some aspirin in the house. Come on, let's go and get it and then you can bring me to Erich.'

With great haste, we rush over to my apartment. I pray that the aspirin I saw not long ago in the bathroom cabinet is still there. Samuel waits outside while I run up the stairs to the bathroom. I search the cabinet until I eventually find the little glass bottle with the faded label. Luckily Frau Werner is not at home. Does the end justify the means in this case? Medicine is scarce and stealing it is no minor offence. But then I see Samuel's desperate face in my mind, and think of gentle, sweet Erich, and put the bottle in my pocket without further hesitation.

We can hear the chanting even before we enter the House of the Templars. Erich is laid out in the middle of the fireplace room. Candles have been lit and everyone is standing around him. It's an eerie scene that reminds me of Caravaggio's painting of Lazarus, which we studied in the preliminary course. It looks as if everyone is pulling at Erich, and there's an acrid smell in the air of bitter herbs, alcohol and sweat. Samuel pushes his way through the throng. I follow him and am shocked by Erich's appearance. His shirt is completely soaked in sweat, his skin shimmers with a blueish hue. Now and again, he lets out a groan and thrashes about. Sidonie stands at the head of his bed, wiping his forehead with a damp cloth.

'We've managed to find some aspirin,' says Samuel.

'Completely out of the question,' she says.

'But Sidonie, we can't just ...!' Samuel looks at her imploringly.

Sidonie doesn't even look up. She carries on doing what she's doing, which seems pointless to me. She wrings out a new cloth, pulls up a bucket of water and wipes Erich's forehead again. Her meticulousness enrages me. I take her hand and pull her blindly behind me out of the building, with Samuel following us.

Once we're outside, Sidonie pulls herself free. 'Can you please tell me why you refuse to give Erich medicine that will lower his temperature?' I say. I'd never have thought I would have the courage to speak to Sidonie in this way.

'Don't pretend you're interested in Erich's health all of a sudden. You lost the right to be involved in matters here long ago,' says Sidonie, and shakes her head.

'But Sidonie, if we already have the medicine ...' Samuel interjects. Sidonie turns to him and speaks in an emphatically low voice: 'It's industrial poison. It's what makes people ill in the first place. Our methods are much more effective. Natural herbs, nothing that will contaminate him further. But you know all that anyway.'

'But we've been trying that for three days, and he's still not showing signs of getting better. I so want to relieve his pain.' Samuel has tears in his eyes.

Sidonie puts her arms around him and turns her back towards me a little more.

'Sometimes people just can't be helped. Erich was always a bit different from the rest of us, you know. You see it in his complexion, his teeth, even in his breath. Other races have different ways of protecting themselves from toxins and impurities. Perhaps we'll be lucky, and his body will make it. But perhaps we'll have to let him go.'

Samuel sniffs loudly a couple of times and nods to himself. I can hardly believe my ears. 'You poor fools. You're the ones who can't be helped!' I say, my voice cracking.

I'm about to leave when Frida comes running out of the house. 'He's woken up!' Samuel and Sidonie run back in, but I stay outside, my pulse racing, and stare at the statues over the entrance. At least now I have certainty. Certainty that all their rules, customs and rituals are mere instruments of exclusion. Certainty that my scepticism was justified. Certainty that their worldview, which seemed so attractive to me, is on a collision course with reality, precisely because it is so oblivious to the world.

~

Easter comes and goes. Preparations for the exhibition start to escalate. 'How are we supposed to manage this in such a short time?' is the general grumble heard everywhere. But our nervousness, which often spills over into silliness, proves a great unifier. At some point, I hear from some other students that Johannes has left the Bauhaus for good and that Sidonie, Erich and Samuel have followed him to Switzerland.

The lantern festival is tonight, one of the Bauhaus celebrations I've never attended. A procession of lanterns takes place on Gropius' birthday every year, which of course didn't make it any more interesting to the cowl-wearers. It's a warm but cloudy day in May and Friedrich has arranged to pick me up from Frau Werner's. I haven't worn my monk's robes in a long time, but today I even dare for the first time to put on my summer clothes, which I haven't worn for nearly two years. I dig out a light blue silk dress that I'd completely forgotten about and the shoes my mother gave me for Christmas. After putting on make-up, I take a long look at myself in the mirror. The person staring back seems foreign to me, but also pretty and ladylike.

I feel light and attractive, and anticipation of the evening ahead skips through my body. I wait in the front garden, which to Frau Werner's delight is already flowering. Friedrich's lantern is, of course, a martial red colour, and I can't help giving him a mocking smile. I've chosen an oriental shape, but instead of Far Eastern patterns, I've stuck it with red and blue triangles. We stroll through the warm evening air to the Sternbrücke. Even from a distance, I can see many people standing around on the banks of the Ilm. It's pleasant to look forward to meeting the others, feeling nothing but curiosity and interest, and no longer worrying about judgemental looks behind my back.

Though it's still light out, some students have already lit their lanterns. Others are doing the same as we climb down the steps of the stone bridge. Matchboxes are being passed around, and some of the especially outlandish creations are proving difficult to light. The inventiveness of my fellow students amazes me every time. Some have built enormous papier mâché globes; there is a silver rectangle, a blue ship and even a tiny bird with real feathers. I wonder where they found the time to fit it all in together with the workload for the exhibition. We join a group of Friedrich's friends. Calmly and a little absently, I listen to them chatting until the candles have all been lit and we go to pick up masters Klee, Kandinsky and Schlemmer from their respective homes, which is accompanied by a lot of shouting. The few pedestrians on Weimar's streets eye us with suspicion. Finally, we stand together at Gropius' door. A group of students with musical instruments strikes up a loud, boisterous birthday tune. Gropius opens his door and feigns surprise, but inside his roomy flat are long tables covered with white tablecloths and decked out with food. There is bread, cheese, ham and wine, and in the corner, I spy a cake. No one pretends to hold back: we all head for the buffet platters with huge appetites. The lanterns left at the entrance form a bizarre pile of papier mâché, wire and tissue paper.

I can't remember the last time I spent an evening in such a relaxed mood. I get to know many other students properly for the first time, have long conversations, eat and drink to my heart's content and enjoy the feeling of not having any expectations. The last guests leave around two o'clock in the morning. I stroll through the balmy night, feeling elated, plucking flowers in passing and balancing along the narrow kerb.

22 May 1923

Dear Luise

You mother and I have decided that your residency in Weimar is no longer worthwhile. We have secured you a place at the Pestalozzi Fröbel School in Schöneberg where you will begin your studies in June. Your mother is personally acquainted with Frau Droescher, the director of this excellent housekeeping school. Frau Droescher reassures us that you will feel very comfortable there. Come back to Berlin at once. We will take care of your expenses in Weimar.

Your father

Dessau, 1926

I hear the music in the distance. Our ears are sharper than our eyes, but I can still make out a bright object through the gloom. I walk faster, my shoes crunching through the frozen snow. I see a gigantic, glowing cube, isolated in the desolate landscape, growing as I approach. The light shining through the enormous glass façade dazzles me. The building glistens and hovers, transparent and yet solid. It is an alien object, a luminous spaceship that has landed on earth and now stands upright and white in sharp contrast to the grey snow covering the ground all around.

I walk up to the entrance. It first leads into a smaller section of the building, which is covered in concrete. Seven letters have been mounted on to the exterior, which is partially engulfed in darkness:

B-A-U-H-A-U-S

I stop, my gaze steadfast, my body shivering. What we always imagined now exists, I think, trembling. Our jumble of ideas has manifested in a tangible place. There it is, in front of me, and it can no longer be doubted, rejected or removed from the world. I feel energy well up inside me, unfamiliar because for years I have retreated into a shell of resignation and indifference.

Building a house means creating a world in which people sleep and eat, work and love, argue and organise. A house is not just a place to shelter people: it affects their way of living and thinking. No wonder that the lives of my brother and his friends, and my mother too, are so limited and rigid, stuffy and superficial. Nothing feels more important to me than being here right now, in this place where people understand that we can no longer stay put, but need something new.

I want to build the future and tear down the past.

~

Directly below the letters, a man stands wrapped up in so many colourful blankets that his face is barely visible. A red arrow made of cardboard hangs around his neck, containing instructions printed in lower case: *that way!* When he sees me, he calls out cheerily: 'Not this way, that way!' pointing to the right.

I walk along the shiny façade. Around the corner, another oblong building appears. A connecting wing forms a bridge between the two.

I admire the glass façade, which looks completely stable despite its transparency, stretching over three storeys like a curtain. Under the bridge, there is a large door with a small crowd standing outside. I don't recognise anyone.

I haven't seen Friedrich for three years now, and his letter didn't contain much except for an invitation to the inauguration of the new Bauhaus building. At first, I followed developments at the Bauhaus as best I could in the newspapers – the takeover of the conservative alliance in Thuringia, financial difficulties in Weimar, and finally its relocation to Dessau. Since the move, it's been harder to find out what's going on from a distance. I know that Gropius is still the director, but other than that, I'm not sure which of my old friends I'll meet.

I keep my eyes peeled for Friedrich's red hair, in vain. I stand with my back to the large window next to the chapel and watch the commotion. Just as I decide to at least get myself a glass of wine, I feel a tap on my shoulder: Friedrich laughs with his same throaty giggle, then hugs me. His shock of hair is now neatly slicked back with pomade, a glistening light brown. 'You look so grown up!' I say, glancing at his suit, which is threadbare and has patches at the elbows.

'Oh, I'm just pretending. Come on, let's get ourselves a drink.'

We thread our way through the crowds. Friedrich pulls me by the hand through one of the three doors into an assembly hall, which is packed with people. The chair frames are made of steel tubes, and only the seats and armrests are made of mere fabric. I want to take a closer look at how they're made, but Friedrich presses on. When he clambers up on the stage, I try to hold him back, alarmed. But he shouts something over the din and points behind the podium where three large sliding walls have been moved to one side, revealing the canteen beyond. It is spacious and brightly lit, various colours shine on the ceiling, and many small stools and tables are laid out. There's a service hatch at the far end, where they're serving wine today. It takes ages until we get there. I ask Friedrich how many people have come for the opening. 'Around a thousand, I'm guessing,' he says, his eyes shining.

A gong sounds, signalling the beginning of the programme. I am about to set off for the assembly hall, but Friedrich holds me back. The stage, he explains, is supposed to be like an amphitheatre. Although Gropius didn't get permission to break through the wall to the garden, it's going to be open on at least two sides, and we'll be able to see the event just as well from the canteen. We look around for seats. Friedrich sees a few of his friends at one of the tables near the front. They squeeze in to make room for us. I'm not sure that I think the idea of the amphitheatre works – Gropius, who now steps out on stage to thunderous applause, tries to address both sides of the audience, which results in him talking mostly to the wall in-between.

I'm too curious to listen to the speech. In a whisper, I quiz Friedrich. He's now an assistant in Gropius' architectural office, he says. 'Actually, we've only been working on the buildings here in Dessau for the past few years, but I assume I'm going to be coming to Berlin more often in the next few years. At least I hope so. I'm not sure how worthwhile my work is here with Gropius, and in Berlin, at least I can support my comrades.' I want to ask more questions, but people are starting to give me nasty looks. Gropius, who in his function as the director is just preparing to thank the city of Dessau and introduce the mayor, seems to be in lively spirits, but he looks many years older. Now a good-looking, middle-aged man with a black, gleaming moustache comes on stage.

'That's the man who brought us to Dessau,' Friedrich whispers in my ear. 'Fritz Hesse. He's a German Democrat, but quite all right otherwise.' Friedrich makes me smile. He seems to be still following every move in local politics. The mayor is not unlikable, but he makes the kind of speech only politicians can: much too long, full of repetition, without really saying anything. I look at the struts on the ceiling, which are painted to emphasise rather than hide their structure. The windows also reveal their origin in factories. Everything here is clear and unadorned; everything looks bright and new. I could spend hours just looking at it all. The mayor has finished his speech, and the band comes on stage while the applause is still going on. The respectful silence in the room is broken, the hum of conversation fills the room until eventually a beam of light shines on stage and the talking stops. The spotlight looks for and finds a figure in a silver mask and white costume.

I know this kind of theatre from my Weimar days, but I never had much to do with Oskar Schlemmer and his students. Their first performance took place during the last big exhibition in the summer I had to leave the Bauhaus. At the time, I locked myself in my room in Berlin for three weeks, thinking in despair about the celebrations, my friends and everything I was missing out on – until my father eventually put his foot down and forced me to take part in everyday life. The mute actor moves back and forth between the metal sliding walls like a gymnast. He dances like a somnambulist, and his costume – two cones for legs, a cone for his belly – gives him a disembodied look. After a few minutes, I can only make out objects wandering through black space. 'Schlemmer invented something you might call architectonic dance,' Friedrich explains quietly. 'The dancers represent the axes in the surrounding space.' The performance doesn't last long but earns the loudest applause so far. Then Gropius steps on to the stage again for a moment and explains that the masters' houses and new students' residences are open for viewing the following day before he says a few closing words.

'Enough with the programme!' one of Friedrich's friends says. 'Let's go to the house. Are you coming?' I look at Friedrich, puzzled. 'The Prellerhaus; that's where we live now.' When he sees that I'm even more confused, he adds: 'We just named the student residence here after the one in Weimar.' The others have already disappeared into the crowd. Friedrich keeps stopping and talking to people. Finally, we arrive outside in the cool air. To the right, a further staircase leads to the residential wing. I hear voices coming from the stairs. Apparently, we're not the only ones who have left the party. On the fourth floor, we walk down a long corridor where all the doors are ajar. Friedrich's friends have gathered in one of the rooms. One is sitting on the bed, the others have made themselves comfortable on the floor. Despite being Gropius' assistant, Friedrich's social skills haven't improved: he forgets to introduce me and falls longways on to the bed. The tall, slim man sitting on the only chair in the room, who introduces himself as Josua, obviously has better manners. He stands up and offers me his seat. The chair is also made of steel tubing and is covered with a finely woven fabric that looks like it was made in the weaving workshop. It's surprisingly comfortable.

'Which one of you lives here, anyway?' I ask, looking around the room. It's untidy, with open books and note-pads lying everywhere, but strangely, it still seems orderly. Through the large windows, I can see out into the expanse of darkness; and even here, I notice details – the door handles, the window frames, a gadget to open the upper window – that look like they're straight from the factory. I can't believe that only one person lives here. I guess that the room must be at least 65 square feet, which would have been an unheard-of luxury in Weimar. 'This is my humble abode, and Friedrich lives next door,' says Josua. He must be in his late twenties, has dark-brown hair and wide-set eyes. Friedrich's friends bombard me with questions. I enjoy the attention I receive as a student at the original Bauhaus, as well as the only woman in the room. It's as if the air in the room has changed since I entered it. After three dull years at a girls' school, punctuated by the occasional rendezvous with a man my mother thought suitable, I feel very flattered by their interest.

At first, the punchy witticisms and backspins in the conversation are too much for me, but then my mind gets up to speed. I pitch in with sharp retorts – or so it seems to me. The discussion revolves around local politics, the architecture critics who were spotted at the opening cere-mony, and the kind of coverage they expect. 'I thought I saw Fritz Stahl from the *Berliner Tageblatt*,' says Josua. 'I can't imagine he'll write anything too positive,' says Friedrich. 'He always refers to us as "The Modernists". You could take it as a compliment, if it didn't sound so snide coming from him.' Josua nods. 'Hans Natonek was there too.' 'He's from the *Hamburger Anzeiger*, isn't he?' Friedrich asks. 'No, he's now moved to the *Neue Leipziger*,' I say, proud to be able to contribute to the conversation. Over the past three years, I have read everything on architecture I was able to find. I spent hours in the enormous library on Unter den Linden, which houses not only a vast number of books but also journals and dailies. At some point, I knew the names of the art critics from every major newspaper, had my darlings and my foes, but never anyone with whom I could share my thoughts. And here I am, sitting in a room full of people who not only have the same references as me but are even mentioned in the articles.

Josua keeps on fishing out new bottles of wine while he and Friedrich argue ferociously over the German Communist Party; and at some point, I'm so drunk that I can only sit and listen. I don't understand much of what they're saying, but I do get that Friedrich joined them a few years ago, only to leave again recently, and that Josua refers to himself as a socialist Zionist who does not see a future in the party. Most of the others eventually say goodbye. I had planned to catch the last train home to Berlin, but it's way too late for that. Josua and Friedrich both offer me a place to stay. I decide to go to Friedrich's room, where he forgets, of course, to offer me the bed. Lying on a carpet wrapped in a mountain of blankets and carpets, I fall into a dark, dreamless sleep.

~

The train to Berlin sets off with a jolt. I stare out of the window into the dazzling whiteness. In some places, the snow has already melted, exposing grey-brown branches and patches of earth. I slowly replay moments from last night, my book lying open on my lap. I feel like I experienced more than I had in the past three years combined. I think of the stultifying time I spent at the girls' school; the days that always followed the same routine; lessons with Frau Droescher who tried to teach me submissiveness with her pursed lips and scowls; and the dumb geese whose only goal in life was to tie down a man. And I think of the poor guy I left sitting in the Tanzpalais, sneaking out past the toilet and through the kitchen entrance, and I can't help but smile. What wasn't so funny was my mother's disappointed expression when I once again came home earlier than expected. The fact that I wasn't interested in the men she chose for me didn't even occur to her. Instead, she wondered why I was so unpopular. 'Don't always be so bold, Luise,' she'd say. 'Men are afraid of clever women.'

And then, there was the creeping horror once it became clear that my father didn't have long to live. He had his first heart attack at Christmas, almost exactly a year ago. He got up from the table, looked at his silent family with a serious expression and just keeled over. He fell in a strangely soundless way, his head striking the heavy, soft carpet. Then shortly before New Year, the cough began. It was a sound that I got to know in all variations: congested, spasmodic, desperate, wheezing, croaking, weak – and finally, so deep in his lungs that it was barely audible. It was as though a creature had settled inside his chest, a parasite that he was determined to cough up through sheer Prussian diligence. I'd never had very tender feelings towards my father; his stern, statesmanlike manner simply didn't allow for it. As he grew weaker, my strongest feeling towards him was outrage, both at his inability to fight his illness with his ideals and that he had become living proof of how flawed his principles of honour, virtue and duty were. I was also outraged that he refused to put his work aside, soon stopped coming to the table for dinner, and barricaded himself in his room instead where he would spend the night coughing. And most of all, at the fact that he would leave my mother and me alone with Otto.

When I unlock the front door of our flat, the stagnant air of grief hits me, the inertia that fills my home. Lore does her best to keep up a daily routine. Every morning, she puts out breakfast for us, which is hardly touched. She also fetches flowers from the market like my mother used to do on Saturdays, and distributes them all around the flat. But it's as if my father's frugal spirit, which was always countered by my mother's exuberance, lives on in these rooms, stronger than ever. Otto has taken on our father's business affairs and is on a trip to introduce himself to the trade partners. He'll be back by Christmas at the latest when he will occupy my father's study and transform into just the kind of brutish patriarch he always aspired to be. Before that happens, I have to get out of here. I can't crash at Charlotte's any more: she eventually gave in to one of her admirers – an immensely wealthy, lively American dandy – and emigrated with him to the United States just under a year ago.

I knock on my mother's bedroom door – no answer. I carefully push down the door handle. The heavy curtains are drawn. Strips of pallid December light fall through the cracks. My mother has lost weight, she almost disappears among the big pillows and covers.

'My child,' she says and smiles wanly. Her breath smells of the cognac that she first drank instead of lunch, and now drinks instead of breakfast. I sit on the edge of the bed.

'Mama, shouldn't you get some fresh air? Or drive out to the countryside? It did me a lot of good to get away for a few days.'

'Oh, not really. I have everything I need here,' she says.

We sit in silence. After a while, I say: 'Do you need me here, then? Otto is going to be around much more. Dessau was so nice, and I thought . . .'

'Dessau? What did you do in Dessau?'

'I went to the Bauhaus opening, remember, Mama? They unveiled their new building. We talked about it for a long time before I went.'

I don't know if it's the cognac or grief, or which would alarm me more, but my mother is very forgetful at the moment. However, it's a new, deeply disturbing thing altogether that she doesn't even notice when I've been away for a couple of days.

'Mmmm,' she says vaguely.

'I have to do something with my life. They have the council's support in Dessau. They've built a wonderful building with student residencies and workshops. It's a new development.'

'But you've already studied, Luise.'

'I didn't graduate from the Bauhaus. I had to return to Berlin. I would love to finish what I started. Will you let me?'

'I don't know. Talk to Otto about it when he's back.'

That, of course, is completely out of the question. My brother would never let me go, even if it was just to spite me. But if my mother concedes, I can at least try to get a place at the Bauhaus and present it to him as a fait accompli. I'm not even sure, though, whether Gropius would let me back after such a long time. But my life in Berlin is too desperate not to try.

'I'll talk to Otto. But *you* wouldn't mind, right?'

Her weak nod makes me doubt that she has even understood what we're discussing. With the distinct feeling that I've done something shameful, I leave her alone and sit down to write a letter to the Bauhaus.

~

The acceptance letter comes just in time, on the third Sunday of Advent, a week before Otto is due home. My only chance is to leave right now. I hastily make all the arrangements for my departure and telegraph Friedrich to ask if I can stay with him until I've found an accommodation of my own. It all happens so quickly that I hardly have time to feel happy. Only when I walk through the snow along the long road from the station to the Bauhaus – this time with a heavy suitcase in tow – does my guilty conscience give way to uncontained joy. All the tension falls away as if I have just dodged a terrible future. And somehow, it's true too.

Friedrich is waiting for me at the entrance to the Prellerhaus. I have to ask him to take my luggage, which he does, but only after pointing out that the staircase is painted in primary colours. And it's true: I look up through the angular stairwell at the floors above and see that each storey is painted a different colour. My eye skips from blue to red to yellow, higher and higher. These are the kind of elements that matter to me – small indications that the designer thought out everything down to the last detail.

We spend the evening talking. As usual with Friedrich, the conversation is lively, even if I can't tell him what's going on in my mind, because he isn't interested in things as banal as emotions. The next day, he leaves to spend the Christmas holidays with his parents in Westfalen. The campus goes quiet. I go on long walks through Dessau, which alternately seems like an imperial city and a post-apocalyptic waste-land. I admire the Törten Estate and the masters' houses, which were both constructed at lightning speed by Gropius. The estate, with its enormous collection of small, flat-roofed houses and the rigorously designed, splendid villas of the masters' houses look like smaller versions of the university. Dessau is so provincial that the Bauhaus buildings don't have to fear competition from ornate turn of the century buildings, as they would in Berlin.

I take turns between two cheap pubs in town for my meals, because the Bauhaus canteen is closed. I spend Christmas Eve in Friedrich's room, staring out of the window and across the small balcony into the distance. I feel lonely, but this new environment is too stimulating to be debilitating. Three days after Christmas, an enraged letter from Otto arrives, in which he accuses me of having abandoned our mother, and threatens to cut me off without a penny. I hadn't expected any more money from him, but his allegations about our mother hurt me. I am worried about her.

It's cold in the Prellerhaus, and even though I throw Friedrich's carpet over my blanket, I still get sick just after New Year's Eve. I sleep so much that I lose all track of time. Sometimes when I open my eyes, I can't tell if it's dusk or dawn. The dreams that come with my fever are realistic and violent. There's always someone coughing, spitting blood and twisting in pain, but it's never my father. Bizarre images of huge banquets of food appear in my dreams: Lore's roast joint of pork appears alongside Charlotte's appetizers and Sidonie's bitter root juice. When I open my eyes again, the fever must have subsided because my senses feel sharp again. I hear voices in the corridor and suddenly feel ravenous. Swaying slightly, I stand up and slip my clothes on, then stagger out of the room. I must look terrible because the students I meet on my way stare at me in alarm. The canteen has opened again, the semester holidays are over. I must have slept for days.

After wolfing down a potato soup, burning my lips several times in the process, I feel sick. Quickly, I go out, grip the bannister of the stairs and draw in the ice-cold air. After a few breaths, my nausea subsides. I look up and take in my surroundings for the first time in a while.

A few students stand next to me, smoking. If they are surprised that I ask them what day it is, they don't show it. When I enter Friedrich's room again, he is standing in the middle of the chaos and looking around, baffled. I try to explain, but he interrupts me, orders me back to bed and comes back ten minutes later with a herbal tea. I am astounded by his care and comply gladly.

~

Over the following weeks, I have a familiar feeling: daily life begins for everyone but me. I think back wistfully to my easy-going time when I started in Weimar. Everything was arranged for me, and all I had to do was wait until I was allowed to start the preliminary course. Now I'm broke, have no place to live, and am shocked at my nerve. Have I made a terrible mistake? Even if I'd like to ask my mother for advice right now, I've forfeited that possibility. I've backed myself into a corner with my hasty departure, and now there's no going back. I think of resourceful Maria and try to imagine what she would do.

Money means independence, I tell myself, as I stand in front of the pub where I ate my meals in the first few weeks. A sign by the menu at the door says WAITRESS NEEDED and it's been hanging there for quite some time. I'm in luck: the owner, a morose man with a ruddy complexion, happens to be there and agrees to see me. He doesn't ask about my previous experience as a waitress; instead, his eyes travel slowly and lecherously up and down. 'A nice girl like you wants to work as a waitress, huh?' He has a strong Saxon accent. I say nothing and nod. He blinks at me suspiciously for a long time, then says: 'Well, you can start tomorrow. But you're not to put on any airs and graces, d'you hear?' I nod again quickly, feeling degraded and disgusted, and once I'm back out in the fresh air, I have to take a few deep breaths.

Over the next few weeks, my first impression of the

owner pales. It turns out that he not only likes to undress women with his eyes but indulges his authority over the waitresses by pinching their bottoms and making lewd jokes. And he hates the Bauhaus: 'Crazy pack of Bolshevists,' he spits fervently. Clearly he's hired me to get his fleshy hands on a student from the place he despises.

The search for a flat takes time, but through Friedrich's friends, I eventually manage to rent a small worker's abode not far from the centre of town. It's cold and dark, and the stale smell of the pub and the owner's remarks follow me all the way to bed. At night, my whole body feels itchy and sometimes, I have to get up and turn on the light to make sure that there are no fleas on me. At night I also think of my mother, who might be going insane with grief and who never begrudged me anything. I simply upped and left her all alone with Otto, who may well be taking out his rage on her. I almost never fall asleep before dawn. Every evening, I swear that I will stand up to the owner and give him such a sassy answer that he'll be dumbstruck. But every day, I hold my tongue.

I have never had to do paid work before, and I find its resemblance to the monotony of my studies at the house-keeping school almost funny. But no matter how much it reminds me of the three dreary years I spent in Berlin, there's a fundamental difference: I know it is only for a limited period. As soon as teaching starts for me too, I will have saved up enough to get by for a semester.

I spend the few spare hours I have with Friedrich and Josua in the Bauhaus canteen or working on my housing estate project. It's a plan for a residential estate right in the middle of Berlin, and I can hardly think of anything else at the moment. Although Josua thinks my project is too grand in scale, he helps me with the technical details, and Friedrich always recommends a few books from the library. When it's quiet in the pub, and we're just waiting for the last guests to leave, I sometimes stand at the bar and draw ground plans for my blocks of flats. I also work on a financial plan, calculating the differences in price between various materials for hours. My greatest challenge is finding a way to give every resident equal access to natural light and green spaces. Although I'm designing different kinds of flats – some are for large families, others for the elderly or couples without children – I try to be fair to everyone. I keep dismissing ideas until I find out about the architect Theodor Fischer and his housing project in Munich. The 'Alte Heide' buildings are narrow, long and positioned diagonally to the street. The design gives all the residents the same light conditions and the same access to the garden. At that point, I throw all my old plans away, and in three nights, I draw up new ones with trembling hands.

My relative poverty doesn't bother me. On the contrary, I feel a new kind of belonging, because the students around me have never had much money. When I try to talk to Friedrich about this, he congratulates me on my new working-class status with a sarcastic smile. 'You must feel unbelievably exotic, Luise.' But a month later, when I have my own money in my hand for the first time, I feel proud of myself. Otto, in the meantime, has given up his attempts to order me back to Berlin. His letters let me know that I'm not worth wasting his energy and concern on. One day, a letter from my mother arrives containing fifty Reichsmarks and her best wishes. I'm relieved that she seems to be feeling better and doesn't blame me.

~

Getting an audience with the head of the university isn't as straightforward as it used to be back in Weimar. Friedrich, who works with Gropius and so is highly informed, tells me when the director is in town and when he might have time. I'm determined to get into the architecture department, which is set to open at the beginning of next semester, and I can't think of any other way to do it than approaching Gropius himself. What's more, I've heard that a room is going to open up at the Prellerhaus, and that would solve at least one of my many problems. Friedrich persuades me that the best way to go about it is to turn up at Gropius' office unannounced between two appointments. The office is located in the middle of a concourse and has two doors: one that leads directly into his room, and another to the secretary's lobby. I pray that I'm not about to burst in on an important meeting and open the first one.

Gropius is mulling over some plans and looks up in irritation. Then a good-natured smile spreads across his face. He remembers me and seems genuinely happy to see me. Strangely, his office is much warmer than the rest of the building. The room smells odd, like a combination of plastic and fertiliser. It must be the Triolin, a new, cheap material I've heard about, which was used to laminate the floor. The director's office in Weimar was only finished after I left, but I've heard it was practically identical to this one. A solid wooden table dominates the room, and next to it stands a sturdy, yellow armchair. Gropius invites me to sit down in it.

'You'll be pleased to hear that the weaving workshop is now run by an extremely competent former student.' I am about to interrupt him to make it abundantly clear that I do not want to go back the weaving workshop under any circumstances when he says: 'Frau Pfister has only been master of the weaving workshop since the beginning of the year, but I have heard that she's worked wonders.'

'Pfister? Maria Pfister?'

Gropius nods unsuspectingly. 'That's right. You probably remember her from your time in Weimar.'

I am so astounded that I need a moment to pull myself together. My friend Maria is now the head of the weaving workshop? How come I haven't seen her? And why hasn't Friedrich told me about this? But then I push aside my questions and try to concentrate.

'To be perfectly honest, the work in the weaving workshop never did much for me. But I heard that there is going to be an architecture department here starting next semester. That's where I'd like to study.'

Gropius' expression changes: he gives me a probing, almost sceptical look. He says nothing. I should have known that this wasn't going to be easy. I pull the plans for my fictitious housing estate in Berlin out of my bag, including a map of the surrounding area and model sketches. As he reaches for them, Gropius' reluctance is palpable. He throws them a cursory look and is about to give them back to me when something catches his attention. He taps on the site plan, frowns and looks more carefully. 'Why have you positioned the buildings this way, Miss Schilling?'

He is testing me, I think. I start to explain enthusiastically. When I start talking about ribbon developments, he looks at me in surprise, and when I mention Theodor Fischer, he seems downright incredulous. All of a sudden, we are engrossed in a professional discussion, debating the potential monotony of row housing, the distribution of light, and finally, cheap materials. Gropius' secretary knocks once to say that there is a phone call. To my delight, he waves her away.

Eventually, Gropius says: 'Well, all right then, Miss Schilling, we'll give it a try. You already finished the preliminary course in Weimar, I believe. So, you should join the third semester of specialist training. There you can learn all about the principles of statics.'

An insanely euphoric sense of pride overcomes me and I start pushing my luck. 'By the way, I heard that a room at the Prellerhaus is going to be vacant . . . ' But Gropius is already elsewhere in his thoughts; as far as he is concerned, our meeting is over. 'Well, you best speak to my secretary. Ilse!' His secretary pops her head around the door. 'Ilse, would you please help Miss Schilling with possible accommodation at the Prellerhaus?' I say goodbye to him and follow the secretary into the lobby.

She clearly thinks she has better things to do, but shuffles her papers around until she finds my file. 'As far as I can see, your parents paid your school fees in Weimar. You rented private accommodation there. And now you want to live in the Prellerhaus?' Her stern expression dampens my excitement. I nod. 'I am afraid that the waiting list is very long. And I'm sure you will understand that there are others whose need is greater than yours.'

I consider explaining my situation to her, but her look is so icy that I decide to fight this battle another time. The most important thing is that I am now officially a student at the architecture department.

~

It's the last Saturday before the semester begins – *my* semester, the one I've awaited for so long. Friedrich's friend Hermann, who I've heard a lot about, is throwing a little party at the Prellerhaus tonight. Shortly before nine, I knock at Friedrich's door and together we walk up one floor. On the staircase, I remember that I wanted to ask Friedrich about Maria. I am about to do so when Hermann appears and greets us. It's difficult to guess his age: his face is plump and youthful, he has large eyes and black hair. He's wearing an expensive, ill-fitting suit that is strained across a small paunch. He welcomes us in with a grand gesture. His room is furnished better than anyone else's I've seen. There is a bar in the corner, displaying golden-brown liquors in glittering crystal decanters; the floor is strewn with carpets, and expensively framed drawings hang on the walls. I even spot a gramophone. Josua is already there, his brown hair looking dishevelled. He's sitting on a steel-tubed chair, one of four owned by Hermann. The desk that comes with the room is covered in a white tablecloth, and has become an altar for candles, bread and cheese.

The mood is silly and hungover. I'm the only one who

didn't drink last night. Josua keeps bursting into giggles for no reason, Hermann flaunts his headache theatrically, and only Friedrich seems not to have any symptoms. I let myself get carried away by the mood: soon it feels as if I had partaken in last night's debauchery. There's much talk about how they're going to take it easy tonight, have an early night so that they're bright-eyed tomorrow.

'But you, of course, get a drink,' says Hermann and sets a heavy glass of whisky in front of me. Where he managed to get the ice cubes is a mystery.

'Hermann! Don't tempt me!' mumbles Josua, sinking further in to his chair.

'Let he without sin take the first shot,' Hermann replies and pours three more glasses. His gestures are grand, careless expressions of generosity. We gather around the table to eat and drink. It has been a while since I saw such a varied cheese platter.

When there's a short break in the conversation, I say, 'Friedrich, why didn't you tell me that Maria's still here? As a workshop mistress, no less.'

Everyone stares at me in surprise. 'You know Maria?' Friedrich asks. Only now do I realise that my friendship with Maria had already painfully fallen apart by the time I got to know Friedrich in Weimar.

'She lives right above me,' says Hermann, 'but Frau Professor rarely indulges in earthly pleasures.' There is an element of respect to his mockery, and when I suggest inviting her down, they are all delighted. I feel as if I am setting off on a mission, sent by my team, as I run up the steps two at a time. It's not until I reach her door that I remember the difficulties in our friendship and start to doubt whether she'll be pleased to see me.

Maria's expression is very serious when she opens the door. But when she sees me, her familiar, good-humoured smile lights up her face. She is much thinner, her large watery eyes bulge slightly, but she is still very pretty. After a long hug, she makes me come into her room and tell her everything. I sum up the past few turbulent months, then I ask her if she would like to join us down in Hermann's room. She looks at me with a smile that is both friendly and sarcastic, and says: 'The communists, eh? I have some work to do.' But in the end, I manage to persuade her.

We are welcomed enthusiastically and I can sense that Maria likes the mood. She immediately pounces on the cheese, which reassures me: at least she still loves her food. The conversation jumps nimbly from one subject to the next, drinks are constantly poured, and the resolution to have an early night is imperceptibly replaced by a determination to get as drunk as possible.

Hermann seems to be interested in everything. He's read something on every subject, recalls quotes and figures, and the more the evening progresses, the more attractive I find him. We get on to the subject of Weimar and what has changed in the meantime. Friedrich, Maria and I talk about our experiences like old veterans. Hermann says, 'I imagine the worst thing was all that esoteric nonsense, those freaks who cut themselves off from the world and ran about at Mr Itten's heels like dogs.'

Maria glances at me and says: 'You should ask Luise about that. She spent some time with Itten's entourage.'

I feel betrayed and try to play down my involvement with them. Then I change my mind and say: 'I haven't had anything to do with them for a long time. But they taught me a lot.'

'Really?' says Hermann and raises his eyebrows. 'Like what, for example? How to brew bitter tea?'

As casually as possible, I say: 'I already knew how to do that. It's true that many of their doctrines were far-fetched. But I believe that you can't explain everything rationally. Some people try to force an order on the world and put a pretty bow around it because they're afraid.'

'But that's exactly what they were trying to do. They wanted to tidy up the world according to their rules, chop everything into easily digested pieces, only to despise it or put it on a pedestal. In that way, they're not much different from the far right.'

Now Josua has his say: 'Sorry, Luise, but Hermann's right. That kind of mystic nativism is a pretty natural breeding ground for anti-Semitism.'

'But not all these groups are the same!' I protest. 'Many of my friends in Weimar were Jews.'

Hermann dismisses my remark with a wave of his hand and says: 'Well, they make it very easy for themselves with their intransigent mindset.'

'But they're not the only ones. Technological utopians, fanatics of the Enlightenment, even Marxists' – here, I throw an apologetic glance at Friedrich – 'can be much worse. They even lay claim to an "absolute truth". At least esoteric groups recognise that certain things are beyond human understanding.'

'Hold on, scientists are supposed to base their research on doubt. They can – are even urged to – make corrections at every stage.'

'But before they make that correction, they already have exactly the entitlement I'm talking about: the fixed idea that, at any given moment, the world can only be evaluated according to the latest dataset.'

It's an intellectual tug of war. Although no one changes their mind in the end, it's fun to rise to the challenge. I could carry on for ever, but the others soon lose interest. Friedrich has been very quiet the whole time. When he finally gets up to leave, it's obvious that he's making an excuse. Josua is busy trying to teach Maria Polish drinking toasts, and eventually, the whole group watches. Then he turns up the gramophone and, with an ironic bow, asks Maria to dance. When I go to join them, I suddenly realise how drunk I am. Hermann takes me by the hand, the room spins, I trip over a chair and all of a sudden, his reddish face is very close to mine. We kiss, we dance, we kiss again and dance again as if to cover up the fact that there's something important happening. I'm not sure how long this goes on for. I blot out the others, intoxicated by the music and the way Hermann is looking at me.

When we finally fall on to the bed, laughing and exhausted, dawn is already breaking through the large, iron-framed windows. I have to go home straight away, I think, but when I start gathering my things, a storm of protest breaks out. 'We'll all stay here tonight, there's enough room for everyone,' says Hermann.

I let him persuade me. Maria somehow manages to break away and leave, Josua has long since fallen asleep on the carpet, so Hermann and I share the bed. When soft snoring comes from Josua's direction, Hermann's kisses become more insistent. He doesn't seem to mind someone else being in the room, but the alcohol and the late hour do their part, and we soon fall into a drunken sleep, tightly wrapped in each other's arms.

I wake up before the others, twist myself out of Hermann's arms and walk barefoot into the kitchenette to splash cold water on my face. I'm still drunk and a headache pounds at my temples. When I go back into the room, both of the others have woken up. Josua presses a pillow into his face, groaning, while Hermann breezes around the room, tidying up, clearing away glasses and finally producing a ceramic, American-style coffee machine. He greets me with a kiss like we've been married for ten years. He goes up to knock on Maria's door, and soon the four of us are sitting on his bed, suffering our hangovers together. Hermann puts his arm around me while Josua lies in the recovery position on his side and Maria has made herself comfortable under the cover at the end of the bed. We remind each other what happened last night, and our excessive consumption of whisky takes on heroic proportions. Any comment is a pretext for us to burst into fits of giggles – Josua's trembling hands as much as Hermann's late-night resolution. We make plans for the coming days: Hermann comes up with ever more fanciful ideas and we laugh at him. I feel unwashed, my clothes are crumpled, and I'm hungry. And still, I think, if I ever have a family, I want things to feel exactly this way.

~

My first lecture takes place in Hannes Meyer's office because the architecture department doesn't have its own classrooms yet. I've arranged to meet Josua but I arrive much too early, and stand around in the long corridor, looking out through the glass façade on to the workshops. I know that I won't be lucky enough to see familiar faces, such as Klee with his huge, dark-ringed eyes, or the distinguished Kandinsky. I wonder briefly whether it was a good idea to skip the introductory course.

Then the other students arrive. Meyer opens his door punctually and asks us in. Except for a few chairs and a table, the room is empty. The walls are bare; no papers are lying about anywhere, not even books. Meyer starts by saying a few introductory words. He has a broad, somewhat thin-lipped smile, is wearing a casual brown suit and talks fast and decisively. He has a Swiss accent, but he makes an effort to speak standard German. Josua arrives late and sits down noisily beside me. Meyer says that one must consider the residents' needs when constructing a building. The sun, the interaction between light and climate, the daily trip to the letterbox or the effect of noise from other neighbours can all be precisely calculated. He doesn't say it straight out, but I have the feeling that he doesn't think Gropius has gone far enough in this regard. I like the way he radically rejects any aesthetic considerations. I think of the icy temperatures in the Prellerhaus in winter, and all of a sudden, Gropius' functionalism seems hypocritical. Meyer is more consistent; he thinks things through instead of wanting to distance himself from decorative effects. I could listen to him for hours, but he keeps it short and then introduces us to Alcar Rudelt, a small man with a melancholy expression who I had taken for a student. He is an engineer from Dresden who is going to teach us the principles of statics.

Meyer leaves, and I spend the ensuing hour in a panic, trying to write down terminology and formulae that I don't understand. Except for a chatty, exceptionally eager young man, who obviously wants to stand out for his grasp of higher mathematics, there is a focused silence. I don't know if I'm the only one who needs to visit the library later on to look up terms such as fixed and floating bearings, paths of contact, traction power, first moments of area and section modulus. At the end of the first lesson, the large sheet of paper that Rudelt has used in place of a blackboard is covered in scribbled equations. For the first time in ages, I feel nostalgic and think back to my father, who could do these kinds of problems in his sleep. I'm sure, however, that he would never have explained them to me. Physics, in his opinion, was not something I should trouble my pretty head with.

~

Over the next few weeks, perhaps spurred on by this thought, I spend every free minute I have in the library. I trawl through reference books until I feel I have mastered the equations. I only do one shift a week in the pub now. This should give me some relief, but instead, the more time I spend in the clean, bright Bauhaus rooms, the more I live in horror of going to a place that stinks of cold cigarette smoke and sour beer. I secretly long for the times when I could rely on a cheque from my parents. At the end of one particularly gruelling shift, Hermann suddenly turns up. His party wasn't that long ago, and although my legs ache and my unkempt hair smells deep fried, I'm happy to see him. The fact that he's found out where I work and simply turns up seems impressively straightforward after my experience with Jakob.

He greets me with a kiss and decides that I need a hot shower and a cup of tea. It's a relief not to have to go home alone to my cheerless little flat and I'm grateful to have Hermann taking care of me. In the Prellerhaus, I stand in the empty communal shower and let the hot water pelt down on my head. Wrapped in a silk dressing gown that Hermann left out for me, I go into his room. Before I get a chance to drink my tea, Hermann opens the belt of my dressing gown with all the awe and anticipation of a little boy opening a present. The poise and self-assurance that made him attractive slip away. His soft, hesitant touch surprises me. Being in his early forties, I assumed he would be much more experienced than someone my age. I sleep with him anyway. My desire feeds off the way he looks at me – a stunned, elated gaze that flatters and relaxes me.

We lie in the twisted sheets, head on shoulder. I tell Hermann about my awful job at the pub. 'You have to leave,' he says with determination. 'The Bauhaus offers guided tours to visitors – you could do that instead.' When I tell him about the presumptuous landlord, he becomes even more vehement. 'Tomorrow, you're going to visit Gropius' secretary and apply for the job.' I'm about to tell him that my first meeting with Ilse Schild wasn't very promising when there's a knock at the door. Hermann shouts out, 'Just a minute!', laughing, and we jump up and pull on our clothes as best we can. As we do so, the door opens, and Josua looks in. Friedrich is with him, but the comedy of the situation seems lost on him, while we gladly suffer Josua's laughter. Once more, I notice how little there is to be ashamed about in their company.

When we are all sitting at Hermann's table, Friedrich, who has just returned from Berlin, reports what has been going on there. He is even paler than usual. 'On Saturday, while we were all here enjoying ourselves, around seven hundred fascists stormed a railway carriage in Berlin and beat up twenty communists,' he says. 'I set off for Berlin the very next morning, our comrades wanted to protest on Wilhelmplatz. The chief constable didn't let us, of course. But we went there anywhere. The cops just fired into the crowd, we hid behind cars, but at some point, we had to run for it. I later heard that one of our comrades was hit.' He buries his head in his hands, then looks up in desperation and says, 'It can't go on like this!'

Josua pats him on the shoulder. Hermann says: 'They're only trying to get attention, Friedrich. You shouldn't give it to them.'

'What else are we supposed to do? Sit around here in our workshops discussing things? Drawing plans? No, the real struggle is elsewhere. You have to understand that.'

I have never seen Friedrich so worked up.

'I've decided to stop working for Gropius. I'm moving to Berlin. We can't leave the battlefield to them.'

'But Friedrich, Berlin is full of communists; what are you planning on doing there anyway? Isn't it better if you focus on creating living space for workers?' Josua asks.

'Well, that's typical of you, making sure you're safe from the real struggle! You didn't even stay in Palestine!' yells Friedrich.

'I don't know why you're attacking me. That's exactly what they want us to do. And besides, you don't need to act like this. All you've been doing is working for Gropius the whole time.' I can see that Josua is livid, but his voice is steady.

Hermann says: 'The far right is doing a good job. Now they're in the newspaper, and we're sitting in Dessau talking about them.' He looks amused, which infuriates Friedrich.

'And you find that funny! Well, of course, you would, with your bourgeois ambitions. You probably even sympathise with them secretly. I remember the way you defended Strasser last year.'

Hermann's grin persists. 'Friedrich, perhaps you should just calm down for a minute; the class struggle isn't going anywhere fast.'

Friedrich goes as white as a sheet. All of a sudden, he stands up and says through gritted teeth: 'Go ahead, stay in your ivory towers! I don't want to have anything to do with this.' He knocks over a chair in his way and leaves.

Silence. Hermann and Josua look at each other and start giggling at the same time. I feel uneasy.

'Shouldn't we go after him?' I ask.

'Nonsense,' says Hermann, 'he'll calm down.'

'But what if he does hand in his notice with Gropius? Apart from that, perhaps what he's saying isn't so far from the truth . . .'

'A-ha, so my little Luise wants to be a revolutionary?'

Hermann asks sarcastically, taking my legs and putting them on his lap.

'It's incredible that he accused me of leaving Palestine,' says Josua. 'He knows that I'm going back as soon as I've finished my studies here. But without training, I'm no use to anyone there.'

'Oh, don't take it too seriously,' Hermann says. He gets up and fetches the decanter of whisky yet again. 'Let's have a drink and work out how we can get Luise a job giving guided tours at the Bauhaus.'

~

I do get the job. Both Hermann and Josua put in a good word for me with Gropius' secretary. I imagine that their opinions carry some weight, because they've both been studying at the Bauhaus for some time now, but I don't ask. My life improves straightaway. The tour groups that visit the Bauhaus are all interested, open-minded people, mostly from Berlin. I am proud to be a student at a university so famous that people come all the way to Dessau to see it. I hardly spend any time in my flat, because most of the time I am with Hermann, who even makes a key for me. At first, I'm baffled by his loyalty, but then I start to get used to it. He never seems to question for a minute that we are a couple. We see each other almost daily and he's always buying me thoughtful little presents, and proudly introduces me to everyone we meet. The contrast to my doomed relationship with Jakob couldn't be greater.

Maria spends most of her time in the weaving workshop. When we finally get a moment to have a quiet conversation, the weather has already turned summery. The balconies, which hang like small baskets on the façade of the Prellerhaus, have become the centre of all activity. It is a sunny, warm day in June, and we're sitting on the concrete floor, our legs dangling through the railings. Maria is more serious than she used to be. She is overworked, and her cheerful nature is buried beneath the resulting tension. I am a little nervous in her presence, but Maria doesn't seem to hold any grudges from the times when our friendship broke down in Weimar. She lets me talk for a long time about Hermann. My newfound love still strains my credulity. Then the conversation turns to Jakob, and all at once we're talking about the old days. I tell Maria about my dramatic departure from the Itten group, and she tells me about the exhibition which I only just missed.

'Do you know what Sidonie is doing these days? Or Jakob?' she asks.

'No. I guess they're still in Switzerland, bathing in spa waters.'

'I'm glad you came to your senses at last. That kind of group dynamic can be dangerous. Always is. You don't have to go along with everything, Luise, just because people ask you to. Be a bit more careful this time.'

'You mean, with the boys here? They seem harmless to me.'

Maria has always been someone who knew all sorts of things about all kinds of people. I wonder if there's something she's not telling me.

'What have you heard?' I ask.

She gives me an odd look, starts to talk, then seems to

think better of it, before saying: 'Yes, I think they're all pretty decent. People say that Hermann is a real womaniser, but he seems to have fallen in love with you.' When she sees that she's making me uneasy, she adds: 'It's probably just because Josua told me Hermann once ran off with his girlfriend. Don't worry about it.'

I'm not exactly sure what to make of this news. Although I find Hermann attractive, I always thought I was the only one who felt that way about him – in comparison to Jakob he isn't a conventionally handsome man. I think of the argument with Friedrich and sense that these men are not very good friends to each other. But then I think of their familial coexistence, which must come from a deep trust. Perhaps they are more generous with their forgiveness than other people. In any case, whatever problems they have, it has little to do with Hermann and me.

I change the subject and ask Maria what she's doing in the weaving workshop. I can tell it's important to her. She sounds so competent, the way you only can if you're so deeply involved in your subject that you don't even notice how many facets of it require explanation. I admire her, not just for being so good at her craft, but also for having an entrepreneurial approach. And clearly, she's successful. The textiles workshop, she tells me, is the only profitable workshop at the moment. 'It drives me mad – everyone is pretending that advertising is the most important thing. But the best ads won't take us a step further if we don't have anything to sell. The architecture department doesn't produce a single thing, but the entire teaching here is now geared to the grand students of architecture!' She stops for a moment and says: 'Sorry, you're one of them too now.' I shrug it off. Maria hurls a stream of invective at Gropius that is so funny in its spitefulness that I can't help but laugh. Maria joins in laughing. 'It's true,' she says, unable to maintain her fierce expression.

~

The library, which is little more than a small room on the third floor, is dusty and mostly empty. I sit on the floor, magazines and books piled up around me. This morning, the file of the plot in Berlin that I ordered finally arrived. I also had them send me excerpts from the land register, although I have decided to ignore the real ownership status for the time being. As megalomaniacal as my plan is, I don't imagine being able to actually build this housing estate in Berlin. But I would like to be able to present an idea that fits the topography of the area. I want to prove that I have considered all eventualities.

In the current issue of *Bauwelt*, I come across an article that mentions the 'Alte Heide' housing project in Munich, which interested me so much a few weeks back. In search of more technical details, I continue to look through the journals. It's like detective work, jumping from one article to the next, getting engrossed, coming up with new questions and trying to answer them. I don't follow any particular system, I simply amass as much information as possible, in order to be able to answer my first question: how can one plan a housing estate on a particular site in such a way that individual building components can be reproduced at a low price, while still offering residents a high standard of living?

The answer to the first part is not very hard to find, at least in concept: Gropius has provided the answer in the form of the Törten Estate.

In the black leather-bound notebook that Hermann has given me, I write a list of requirements for my building: *brightness, comfort, short distances, storage space, latest technology*. The July sun glares through the large windows of the library, making the small room stuffy, and my head starts to pound. I think of the others, who have taken a walk to a small lake and only left me behind after staging a small protest. I continue my list in sweeping handwriting: *heat and cold insulation, ventilation*. I leave out aesthetic elements: whether someone has a preference for high ceilings is not important to me. Then I order the list according to priorities. In the end, *brightness* and *ability to regulate room temperature* are at the top of the list, *the latest technology* at the bottom. I look at my old building plans and am happy to see that everything is falling into place. On one plan, I have drawn a rectangular, very narrow building, and I now align the bedroom eastwards and the living room westwards. This way, the residents will wake up and have dinner facing the sun.

I'm also working on the tasks that we've been assigned in class, of course. We're mostly learning about statics. We do a few analyses of existing buildings, examining the relationships between neighbours on a housing estate according to given criteria. But these constant comparisons don't go far enough for me; I want to design something big, something that can be reproduced and have long-term effects on the construction of housing estates. Perhaps Josua is right, and I overestimate myself. Then again, all the buildings and housing estates that I admire for their modernity and practicality were designed by human beings.

~

The windows in the Prellerhaus are like magnifying glasses for the July sun: I wake up dazed, in a complete sweat. Once again, I have been drinking until the early hours – partly because the conversation was so interesting, and partly because I was trying to keep up with Hermann. He's no longer next to me in bed. I go out on to his small balcony and see him down on the grassy bank in front of the building, doing gymnastics exercises with Josua and a few other students. The sports craze that seems to have caught on everywhere was strange enough back in Weimar. At least here in Dessau, no one tells me I have to join in. Besides, it's a lot more pragmatic: sport here isn't used to set a few people apart from those who are less fit, nor is it linked in some mystic way to nature.

The gymnasts don't notice me. I admire Josua, who does the exercises smoothly and effortlessly with his tall, thin body. Then I see Hermann giving a piggyback to a pretty girl with short, dark hair, and what Maria said crosses my mind. I feel a strong twinge of jealousy, but I manage to control myself. Back in the room, I make coffee and even though there is no one watching me, I get dressed with exaggerated calm. A little later, we're all sitting at a long table on the terrace. Hermann has showered and smells of curd soap and his expensive aftershave. The girl has joined us too, but Hermann sits down next to me and pulls me gently on to his lap, which makes me feel ridiculous about being jealous. The girl seems to be in the fine arts faculty. In any case, they are talking about Klee, and how he's become more and more withdrawn. Kandinsky isn't teaching as much either. The girl is saying that she doesn't think it's right for Gropius to assign these great artists to the scrap heap. But Josua and Hermann don't agree – they think her concerns are exaggerated.

'They get a decent salary, and the masters' houses aren't exactly hovels – it's their fault if they don't get more involved,' says Josua.

I'm secretly glad that they disagree with the girl's views, but I'm surprised at how little I know about the in-house fights at the Bauhaus.

Miss Schild, Gropius' secretary, who is known as 'wild Ilse' for no apparent reason, marches over to us quickly. There is an international call for Josua on the line. It's quite unusual for her to leave her office because of a student's phone call, so we all take notice. We look uneasily at each other until Josua disappears with Miss Schild. Although we should be going to our workshops, Hermann and I decide to wait for him.

Hermann talks about his latest project. It is the third project he has obsessed over since I've known him. He follows a plan non-stop for two or three weeks only to abandon it in the end. Although I don't take his flashes of inspiration quite as seriously as I used to, I enjoy listening to him. He wants to design a new font for the International Phonetic Alphabet. He tells me about a French linguist who invented the alphabet many years ago. Once again, I'm astounded at how eclectic his interests are.

Now he changes the subject to a passion that he has held for quite some time – the psychology of advertising. 'You only have to walk down the main high street in Berlin to realise that people are overwhelmed by it all,' he says. 'There are posters everywhere demanding that you buy something. That's the American style of advertising. German ad men have adopted their style without considering our particular mentality. Americans are more progressive in many ways, but that doesn't mean you can ignore national habits. Domizlaff says that you have to constantly build confidence in a brand instead of reminding people it's there.'

Hans Domizlaff is the ad man behind the yellow posters for Reemtsma cigarettes, and after his guest lecture here last semester, he has become Hermann's idol.

'But aren't you being arrogant to believe that people will let themselves be manipulated, just like that?'

'I wouldn't call it manipulation, it's a strategy. If you're trying to sell a product or an opinion, you have to have a strategy – and it doesn't even have to be particularly subtle. People are stupid, Luise, don't underestimate that.'

I'm about to disagree when Josua returns. His forehead is speckled in tiny beads of sweat, and he stares into space. It takes us a while before he tells what has happened. There's been an earthquake in Palestine. His friend's kibbutz east of Haifa has been destroyed. Two of his friends are badly injured, and he hasn't received any news about the third. He decides to go to the post office and send as many telegrams as he can. Hermann presses a large banknote into his hand and Josua hurries off. I am not entirely sure what a kibbutz is, but I don't dare ask.

~

The three of us are sitting on Hermann's balcony. Josua is still in shock from this morning's news. For the first time, he tells us more about his friends in Palestine who migrated there from all over Europe. He talks about the hard work in the fields, the large gatherings at dinnertime, the huge, home-built barracks that are no longer standing.

Hermann says: 'It's a good thing. It means you can build something new there when you're back. *Tabula rasa!* Let's have a drink.' He gets up and fetches a bottle of wine. He's always generous, but now I find his behaviour insensitive. I know, by now, that he comes from a rich family. Perhaps his blasé attitude towards human loss, so similar to Charlotte's, has something to do with his background.

When he comes back out into the summer night, he wants to talk about the exhibition in Stuttgart, put together by the Association of Craftsmen. 'Let's all go there together!' he suggests. 'There's no harm in seeing what they have been up to there.' He wants us all to be in a good mood again; I can sense that.

But I can also see that Josua needs to talk, so I carry on asking him questions. He was born in Galicia, which makes me think of Erich, whom the Weimar petite bourgeoisie always called the 'Galician', even though he was neither from Galicia nor Jewish. After the war, Josua's longing for a new beginning was so great that he set off for the Jordan Valley. It was hard at first, even though many of his fellow compatriots were knowledgeable about agriculture. But the soil wasn't fertile, there was hardly anything to eat, and a few of them came down with malaria. He mentions the name of his group: *Hashomer Hatzair.* I try to pronounce it but fail miserably. For the first time this evening, Josua manages something like a laugh.

'We were hungry all the time,' he says. 'We shared everything. Otherwise, we wouldn't have survived our first stint there. In the years that followed, more and more emigrants arrived, and things slowly changed for the better. Sharing was a tradition we kept. There was no private property, and even tools were locked away at night because they weren't supposed to belong to one person.' He glances at Hermann, who is demonstratively not listening, but jumps up instead, fetches the corkscrew, puts it back again, then pulls out his cigarette case and fiddles with his lighter.

I imagine Josua's life in Palestine on barren hills under the burning sun, olive trees scattered across the landscape. 'Do you even feel comfortable living here?' I ask him.

'Well, I'll never get used to the way some people are fixated on property here. But ultimately, I came here to learn how to build lodging for my comrades that suits our way of living. And the teaching here is good. The houses we built so far were only supposed to be provisional, anyway.'

Hermann nods as if to point out that this is exactly what he just said.

'But this year's entire harvest has been destroyed. And I still don't know if everyone has survived.' Josua rubs his eyes so as not to show that they are welling with tears. I try to comfort him, without much success. In the end, he leaves, and Hermann seems relieved. He pours us some wine and wants to start talking about his project again. It's the first night in a long time that I decide to go home to my little flat.

~

Maria buries her feet in the warm gravel and gazes up idly at the shimmering sky. I shield my eyes from the sun and half-heartedly watch Hermann and Josua hitting a tennis ball back and forth. As so often over the past weeks, Hermann and I spent the night drinking and talking into the small hours of the morning, and, as always, after a desperate hour spent thinking about my plans, I have decided to postpone my work until the next day. The River Mulde is broader than the Ilm, and on the outskirts of town, there are even a few beaches where we are completely alone. Hermann and Josua are naked. I am wearing one of Charlotte's old bathing suits, which is both flamboyant and a little old-fashioned, so I'm not entirely comfortable.

As I'm rummaging around in Hermann's large leather bag for my towel, I come across a slim letter covered in tiny handwriting. Resisting my impulse to read it in secret, I call over to him: 'Who's the letter from?'

Hermann and Josua are exhausted and come over to sit down with us on the large blanket that Maria has brought. 'Oh, Friedrich had to share his paranoid fantasies with me again.'

'May I read it?'

'Of course,' says Hermann, and I feel happy and proud that we don't keep secrets from each other.

The letter is muddled, with talk of secret armaments and fascist paramilitary units that are allegedly supported by the

Reichswehr. Friedrich's tone is urgent, verging on hysterical. He writes about a fire in the Palace of Justice in Vienna; it is still not clear who started it, but for Friedrich, it is the most significant sign that civil war is about to break out. The letter ends with an appeal – we mustn't avert our eyes to the truth any longer. Even here in Dessau, at Junker's aircraft manufacturer, secret military exercises with mustard gas are rumoured to be taking place.

I don't know what to make of it all. Has Friedrich gone mad? Or is he right? Surely we would have heard if the Reichswehr had put together an entire army? My lack of sleep and the heat aren't exactly helping me think straight. My thoughts feel like the slippery stones I'm staring at. Hermann is chatting to Maria, so I ask Josua what he thinks. He studies the letter and then says: 'There's probably some truth to it. But that doesn't change the fact that Friedrich sounds pretty confused.'

'Confused? He's completely deranged,' says Hermann, who seems to have been listening to us. 'Mustard gas in Dessau! Utter nonsense!'

'Aren't you worried about him?' I ask.

'He'll be fine. He has his comrades to take care of him,' Hermann laughs. I think of Hermann's reaction to Josua's troubles a few days ago. Perhaps I should go to Berlin on my own to check on Friedrich? But Hermann and Josua know him much better: it's for them to decide. And they don't seem worried, so I calm down a little. We're all going to Berlin during the break, anyway, and I can still see him then.

Hermann and I leave before the others. In the bushes by the river, crickets chirp, and there's a smell of freshly cut grass in the air. After a few yards, Hermann asks abruptly: 'Are you jealous of Maria?'

'Maria?' I think for a minute. Sometimes Hermann's eyes gleam in a strange way when he talks to other girls. It gives me a pang of jealousy for a moment, but disappears just as quickly. I would have never even thought of Maria.

'No, not at all,' I say, but his question itself has made my answer a lie.

Hermann has already moved on to a different topic. He's talking about Hans Domizlaff again, with whom he has recently started a correspondence, and their shared love of America. I have trouble focusing on his monologue. The summer day, which had been rapturously beautiful, now feels oppressive and muggy. The scent from the blossoming hedges is overpoweringly sweet, and our walk back along the dusty path seems to take an eternity. Finally, the Junkers plant stretches out to our left. Smoke coming from the chimney stacks shimmers in the heat. I think of Friedrich's letter again, and Hermann does too because he says: 'Secret armaments! What twaddle. Until a few years ago, we weren't even allowed to build aircrafts. That's the other side of revanchism: the workers suffer too. After the war, a good five hundred men lost their jobs here. At least they're allowed to build non-military planes now, but that still doesn't provide enough work to go around. And since they founded Luft Hansa last year, they have no reason to do any crooked business.' The way he says 'revanchism' reminds me of Otto's constant drivel about Versailles and the 'stab-in-the-back myth', and it shocks me. I give him a sidelong look. Herman is not Otto, I tell myself. Hermann is jovial and loving, and when he says these things, it's because he's thought about it. Perhaps he's even right.

'Why the sombre face?' he asks now but doesn't wait for me to answer. He takes me in his arms and gives me a long kiss.

～

Our new classroom is already in a state of chaos. Calculations and designs are pinned to the walls, crumpled paper is strewn across the floor and the sink is spattered with ink stains. Hannes Meyer hasn't shown up since his introduction. And now he's standing at the front of the class, and there's a mood of strained concentration.

'I hope you've been paying attention over the past few months,' he says in his gentle Swiss accent and beams at us broadly. 'Today I can pass on to you the first commission, one that may well be realised. The chocolate manufacturer Suchard is opening a shop in the centre of Leipzig. Your task is to design the interior and façade. You have until the end of the semester – a month, in other words. Please get into groups of two.' The room erupts in turmoil, students shout out names across the room and split up into twos. I turn to Josua, but he's already paired up with his neighbour. He makes an apologetic gesture. I look around and feel panicked. I've been spending so much time with Hermann that I hardly know any of the other students.

'Anyone left?' Meyer shouts above the din. Hesitantly, I raise my hand. I'm the only one. Meyer says: 'You gentlemen there at the front, would be you be so kind and take on Miss . . . ?'

'Schilling,' I say, feeling myself blush.

' . . . Schilling?'

'We'll take on chicks if we have to,' says the small man in the first row, eliciting some sporadic chuckles around the room. It's Karl, the smart alec who has been trying to draw attention to himself since the first day of class. The other is a quiet, pale boy who I've never noticed before. I don't let on how annoyed I am, take my things and sit down next to the other two.

'Good, now that everyone has settled,' says Meyer, 'I'm going to leave you the site and façade plans, some photographs and the layout. I expect to see your designs by September the first. If you have any questions in the meantime, please direct them to Mr Rudelt or Mr Köhn.'

He has barely left when everyone seizes copies of the plans. Several people leave the room, including Josua and his partner. I wonder why Josua chose a different person so quickly, seeing as I'm the one he spends most of his time with outside of class. What's more, he knows what I'm capable of, unlike Karl, who spends the next half-hour explaining to me how to read the façade plan. Every time I try to interject, he studiously ignores me. The pale boy, whose name is Augustin, listens to Karl, wide-eyed.

Then we get to the design. 'We definitely need a second display area, right next to the counter,' says Karl.

'It's a very small shop,' I point out. 'Perhaps we should do away with unnecessary decoration and build shelves up to the ceiling. Then the top section could be used as storage space and the chocolate could be displayed at eye level.'

'It's not too small! This is where the counter would be

built,' says Karl and draws it directly on to the floor plan. 'The customers have to see what they're buying, Luise. Believe me, I have experience in commercial matters.'

Augustin has remained silent this whole time, but now he agrees with Karl. When we move on to the design of the façade, I am again unlucky and am outvoted by the other two. After trying to contribute my ideas a few times, I give up and listen. I don't want to put my name on this boring, impractical design, but I can't take a stand against Karl on my own. I comfort myself with the thought of my housing estate designs, which I can spend more time on if I don't waste it here.

~

I unlock the door, shake out my wet umbrella and put it into the wooden stand. This makes me smile: only Hermann would think of buying an umbrella stand. I'm happy that, despite my socio-economic decline, I don't have to make too many sacrifices. The guided tour was tough. About fifty book printers from all over the country arrived to look at the Bauhaus workshops. One of them flew into a real rage when I told him that we only use lower-case letters because it saves time and you can't hear the difference anyway. They weren't happy about the plans to economise on personnel either. When I started to feel that I was losing control, I broke off the tour, blaming it on the rain, and escaped to the Prellerhaus.

Hermann is probably in the printing workshop, working on his design for the Suchard sign. Meyer has also announced a contest for the company's advertising, which

Hermann pounced on with great zeal. I make myself a coffee, sit on the bed and stare out at the rain. At least five books are lying on Hermann's bedside table. He reads them with enthusiasm, talks about them for hours, but they often remain unfinished. I take the one lying on the top of the pile. It's a novel with the title *The Tunnel* and underneath is an edition of the journal *Typographic Notes*. I flick through the novel. It's about an American engineer who wants to connect Europe and America via a tunnel under the Atlantic. It seems old-fashioned and slightly spooky. Then I notice a newspaper underneath the pile and pull it out. On the front is printed *The National Socialist* in a sweeping font, and underneath: *Chief Editor: Dr Otto Strasser.* I open it to make sure it is what I think it is. No doubt about it – it's a right-wing national newspaper. Confused, I put it down. Why does Hermann have a thing like this lying around?

I hear him unlocking the door and go to hide the newspaper. Then I change my mind. Hermann is completely drenched. Cheerfully, he cries, 'My darling!', rubs his hair dry with a towel and looks for a clean shirt.

'Hermann, what's this?' I ask, holding up the paper.

He glances over at it and says, 'A newspaper, what else?'

'Do you read things like this?' I ask.

'Yes, why not? *The National Socialist* isn't bad. The editor's brother is called Gregor Strasser. He's an incredibly smart ad man, extremely industrious. He leads the propaganda department for the National Socialists and stands up for the workers, too. He's more of a socialist, actually, than a nationalist.'

'But Hermann, it's full of anti-Semitic statements!'

'Oh, that's not the focus. Also, you can't really leave out the question of Jewish capital while discussing social issues. You're really throwing the baby out with the bathwater if you label every justified criticism as "anti-Semitic".'

'Does Josua know you think like this?'

'I don't know. I also don't care. Whenever these topics come up, the same old knee-jerk reactions are triggered.'

I don't want to seem as if I am reacting in a knee-jerk fashion, but I don't see what Josua has to do with what Hermann calls 'Jewish capital'. I think about Sidonie, whose father worked in a bank. Perhaps there is a grain of truth in what Hermann is saying on an abstract level that I don't understand.

There's a knock at the door. 'Talk of the devil!' says Hermann, opening the door and giving a cheerful bow. I hide the newspaper under a book.

'Ah, you've brought Maria with you!'

'You don't have to talk about me in the third person, Hermann,' says Maria. She laughs, playfully punches his side and shakes out her wet hair. Since Hermann's recent remark, their intimacy makes me uneasy.

'I can't stay long – this design for Suchard is more demanding than I thought,' says Josua, flinging himself down on the bed. He always moves with such grace and suppleness, perhaps because he is so tall and slim.

'How is it going in your group?' he asks me.

'It's awful. Karl and Augustin have the dullest ideas, which they constantly manage to impose on me. And Karl makes mistakes in the static calculations but won't accept it when I correct him.'

'You correct him?' Hermann asks. 'Always so eager, our little Luise.' He giggles.

'That's not true, I—'

'Perhaps you should be more involved, Luise,' Josua says. 'I never see you with Karl and Augustin.'

I laugh bitterly and am about to explain that I'm only allowed to do the legwork, but Maria interrupts me: 'Hermann, are you growing a moustache, by any chance?'

She's right. There's a blueish sheen on Hermann's upper lip. I never notice such things, but now that I look more closely, I also see that he's wearing a new waistcoat and a colourful tie. Hermann merrily puts down the ceramic coffee pot he was filling and digs out four elegant-looking shopping bags. Then he presents his purchases to us at length. I don't say it, but I suspect he's trying to emulate Herbert Bayer. Bayer was still a student during my time in Weimar but has since become head of the print and advertising department. I've only seen him from a distance, but even back in Weimar, his appearance was quite impressive. With his rigorously slicked-back hair and neatly trimmed moustache, accompanied by his fashionably dressed wife, he struts around the university like the sleekest peacock.

～

Josua is standing up front at the lectern, listening, as his partner talks about their plan, which is pinned to the pock-marked wall. His eyebrows are tense with concentration, which looks odd because of his broad forehead. Meyer, Köhn and Rudelt are sitting in the first row so I can't see their reactions to the presentation. The design is good and well thought-out, I think, and I dread the moment I have to stand up at the front with my compulsory companions. Karl is sitting next to me, furiously jotting notes and even scribbling on our plans. Augustin is staring into space, and I'm not sure he's even listening. I pull myself together and think of my plans for the housing estate, which are safely stored in my leather bag. I am hyper aware of their physical presence against my leg, it's as if they're giving off a glow. The plans have reached a stage where I can't make any more progress on my own. I want to present them to Meyer.

Josua now takes over, nervously tugging his fingers through his hair and leaping from the lectern to the designs on the wall to point out various features. When he's finished, the class applauds. The jury is divided and much stricter than I imagined. Köhn, a tubby, jolly man, is lenient as usual, but Rudelt points out a flaw in the construction, and Meyer doesn't find the design radical enough. I'm so tired that the whole scene seems unreal to me, and I'm not the only one. A student sitting in front of me has rested his head in his hands and looks as if he might nod off at any moment. But while the others have worked the past few nights, I've simply been indulging in my ritual late drunken discussions with Hermann.

'Now I would like to invite Mr Stadler and Mr Probst to the front,' Meyer says, 'and Miss . . . '

'Schilling.'

'Ah, yes, Miss Schilling. Please, ladies and gentlemen, the stage is all yours.'

Karl removes Josua's design and fiddles awkwardly with the drawing pins until he manages to fix our plans to the wall. Then he starts explaining them. Augustin stands next to him in silence. When Karl comes to the part about the counter in the middle of the shop, Meyer interrupts him.

'Excuse me, but why do you want to build an extra counter right in the middle of the shop?'

'Putting a display next to the point of sales gives the customer the opportunity to—'

'Gimmickry! The room is much too small for luxuries like that!'

Karl is thrown by this comment but carries on with his explanations. When he tries to find a way to finish, you can hear a pin drop. Meyer is morosely silent. Then Rudelt sets about picking apart our design down to the very last detail. He finds errors in calculations that I hadn't noticed, probably because I was trying so hard to distance myself from the design.

Karl tries to defend himself: 'To be honest, some members of our group lacked commitment.' He glances blatantly in my direction.

'That's enough! We have no time to waste on poor designs. Perhaps the next group has something decent to offer,' says Meyer.

My eyes burn. The worst thing is that Karl is right: if I hadn't been so put off by his smugness, at least some of the calculations might not have been so off the mark. I want to say something, anything to make it clear that the work was taken out of my hands, but I know that as soon as I open my mouth, I will burst into tears. So, I make do with pulling the design off the wall with a rip. I don't hear a word of the remaining presentations. I spend the time left in class thinking up quick-witted, acerbic comments I could have made; then I fantasise about ways to humiliate Karl. In the end, I picture myself running the most successful architect's office in the country, and Karl whining and begging me for work.

When the class is finally over, a cluster of students forms around Meyer. I wait patiently with my portfolio in my hands until all their questions have been answered. Then I stand next to Meyer, who is bending over the winning design, and say: 'Excuse me, may I show you something that I have been working on in my free time?' Without waiting for him to answer, I spread out my Berlin housing estate plans.

After a puzzled look from Meyer, he says: 'In your free time?' and scrutinises the plans. 'So, you want to build an entire housing estate, just like that?'

'Yes,' I say breathlessly, 'using the latest construction techniques. Look, here—'

'You know, I have nothing against students working on their own projects outside of lessons. But I would urge you to familiarise yourself first with the fundamentals,' says Meyer. He smiles politely, folds up my plans and hands them back to me.

I'm too perplexed to answer, and besides, he has already gathered his things and is walking out of the room with long strides.

∼

I don't want to run into Josua in Hermann's room, nor do I want to go back to my dismal flat. I roam aimlessly through the workshop wing, past the loud clattering in the weaving hall – ducking a little so that Maria doesn't spot me – up the stairs where I pause for a moment, despite the deafening noise of the metal saw and the acrid smell of varnish, then carry on up to the second floor. That's where the carpentry workshop is. The transparency of the building, which meant nothing but freedom to me at the beginning, has now become oppressive. Even if I found a place to be alone, I would still be visible from all directions. At least up here, I don't know anyone. Ever since my brief period in the carpentry workshop in Weimar, I haven't held a piece of wood in my hands, and some people throw me some strange looks. I act as I did in Weimar and choose some material and a couple of tools. The repetitive movements of planing and the smell of wood shavings soothe me. I'd forgotten how satisfying it can be to let your hands do the thinking and still be able to produce something. In this case, it is a base for a wooden case that I turn back and forth in my hands, thinking that I might send it to my mother for Christmas.

Slowly I feel ready to see the others. On the way to the Prellerhaus through the canteen, I am reminded of the busy, happy days with Friedrich in Weimar. I miss my innocence during that time, and how open I was to everything.

Hermann is sitting with Josua, as expected, at the long table in his room. 'Here comes my little Luise,' he says, and pulls me on to his lap.

'We were worried,' says Josua, but he winks. He's not taking my disastrous presentation seriously.

'The semester holidays start in a week,' I say. 'Shouldn't we start planning our trip to Berlin?'

'I can't go,' says Hermann. 'And you know why? I've won the contest for the Suchard sign!'

'You didn't tell me that!' shouts Josua. 'Let's have a toast!' He fetches the crystal decanter of whisky that never seems to run dry. I twist myself out of Hermann's embrace and sit down on the empty chair.

'But we wanted to check up on Friedrich in Berlin . . .'

'Aren't you happy for me?' Hermann shakes his head with a laugh. 'Ice cold, this woman.'

'Of course I'm happy for you. But I've been worried about Friedrich. Since his letter, we haven't heard a thing.'

'Oh, come on, we're going to the Poelzig Festival anyway in spring. Our valiant comrade will just have to wait until then.'

I put a hand over my glass as Hermann tries to pour me some whisky. 'At least you'll be coming, won't you, Josua?'

'No time, I'm afraid.' Josua raises his glass. 'To Hermann, the master of advertising and manipulation of the people!'

'I wouldn't wish friends like you on anyone.' My eyes are burning, but I can't tell whether it is from exhaustion or rage. 'I need some fresh air,' I say, grabbing my coat to leave.

In the weaving workshop, I find Maria, who is busy explaining something to a student. I sit on a stool in the corner and gaze at the looms, these powerful machines with fine limbs that jump nervously and rhythmically across the textiles. Then I watch Maria and her student. I admire Maria's authority, which she is so used to, and the relationship she has with her students. I probably lack something – a certain stamina, which Maria has definitely acquired.

When she's finished, she waves to me. I want to tell her

about the presentation, but I can see she doesn't have much time. So I only report on Josua and Hermann's lack of interest in their old friend.

'I wanted to go to Berlin in the semester holidays! Let's go together,' she says. 'I'm meeting Samuel, in case you remember him.'

I am surprised that Maria has kept in touch with him. She explains that she ran into Samuel in Berlin long after he had turned away from Itten's followers, and that they have got to know each other better over the past two years through letters and visits. I briefly wonder if I should find it strange that she has befriended Samuel, of all people, but my happiness wins.

I hardly have time during the next few days to feel annoyed at Hermann, although he doesn't want to let me go to Berlin, of course. I telegraph my mother and Friedrich, clean my flat and pack a small suitcase. Friedrich doesn't answer for a long time, but my mother contacts me straight away. I can hardly believe how well everything is falling into place: Otto won't be in Berlin when I'm there, and despite the brevity of the telegram, I can sense how much she is looking forward to my visit.

~

The train has almost pulled into Berlin's Anhalter Bahnhof, and tears of laughter are running down our faces. Since we boarded, Maria's mood has been as light as in the old days in Weimar. Our shared excitement about travelling to Berlin makes us increasingly foolish, visibly annoying the other people in the carriage, which doesn't stop us making silly faces and cracking jokes. We deliberately provoke the stiffs around us because it's so easy. I unfold my newspaper and hold it up for us both – but upside down, eliciting ill-tempered hisses from nearby. When we climb down the carriage steps, Maria performs such an exaggerated bow in front of the ticket inspector that an old man stumbles over her leg and calls us 'impertinent rascals', which only makes us break out in laughter again. We say goodbye at the underground train station. Maria is going to a bar in Schöneberg with Samuel that evening, and we arrange to meet at Viktoria-Luise-Platz.

I enjoy riding the U-bahn. Finding my way around this city so effortlessly always gives me a feeling of worldliness and superiority. But gradually, I start to dread seeing my mother again. I'm afraid that she won't be well, that it's my fault, and that she'll blame me for running away.

Lore opens the door, greets me with a hug and only reluctantly lets go. I hear my mother in the parlour and am relieved. At least she's no longer barricading herself in her bedroom. Lore takes my suitcase and coat and shoos me into our flat. My mother has put on weight. She suddenly seems very old to me. But she has found her warm-heartedness again, and when she takes me in her arms, it is long and tearful.

Once she has regained her composure, we sit down for tea brought by Lore. I tell my mother about my life, and make everything sound more comfortable, easy and successful than it is. Nevertheless, she looks at me in concern.

'Shouldn't you be looking for a husband instead of wasting your time in Dessau?'

'Why do I need a husband? I earn my own money.'

'But you need someone to look after you, Luise. And if you want to have children, you shouldn't wait much longer.'

'Children are the last thing on my mind right now!' Although it was predictable we would have this conversation, I'm upset that she can't be happy for me.

'Don't be naïve, my child. You're not getting any younger. If you already have such problems finding a husband, it won't get any easier when you get older.'

'Finding a husband is not that difficult.'

'Well, you haven't had much success up to now. Men aren't interested in suffragettes, you know.'

'But I have a man who loves me!'

It just bursts out of me. I had resolved not to tell her anything about Hermann. I just about manage to play down certain aspects of our relationship and make it sound as innocent as possible. My mother shakes her head sceptically. She thinks that Hermann can't be very serious about me if he hasn't proposed marriage yet.

During dinner and on the way to Schöneberg that evening, my mother's words go through my head. Bourgeois values don't apply at the Bauhaus, and it's not unusual for couples to remain unmarried. Nevertheless, Hermann's little gestures of commitment suddenly strike me as suspicious, like a series of unkept promises. What if he really is keeping his options open? What if I have been lulled into a false sense of security, just because he opened his door, his circle of friends and his life to me? Perhaps we should just get married, like every normal couple? Besides, my mother's right about one thing: it's thanks to Hermann I've been able to maintain my standard of living since Otto cut me off without a penny. And after last week, my chances of earning my living as an architect seem very slim to me. What if I am left completely alone in the end, with nothing except a degree in architecture?

Samuel and Maria are already waiting. A tall woman with narrow eyes and high cheekbones stands next to them under the station sign. I give Samuel a long hug. I didn't realise how happy I'd be to see him. He is wearing a glittery jacket, new glasses and looks quite the cosmopolitan, somehow more upright and self-confident than the Samuel I remember. Maria is wearing thick make-up, her large eyes ringed with black eyeliner. But by far the most extravagantly dressed is the other woman, who introduces herself as Else von der Vogelweide, embracing me without hesitation. The three of them are in the best of moods. Samuel and Maria hook arms with me, and we stroll through the autumnal evening over to Lutherstraße. We arrive at the Eldorado, a cabaret bar with a façade that doesn't look like much from outside. Inside, however, there's nothing discreet about it. Lewd paintings hang on the walls in the corridor, the enormous ballroom is packed beyond capacity, and the air is humid and full of anticipation. Heavily made-up faces glide by, glittering costume jewellery, dangerously short skirts, women in tailcoats and tuxes, men in evening dresses and half-naked boys who might also be girls. It is all very strange to me, and the lascivious mood feels threatening. I want to leave straight away and go home. But something about the mood of abandon fascinates me too, so I entrust myself to Maria, who grabs me by the arm and drags me along.

Samuel is as thoughtful as ever. First, he organises a table, then champagne. There's something to celebrate, he shouts to me over the noise. Else today received permission from the police authorities to wear women's clothes in public. She had waited almost four months for that letter. I try not to show my surprise. Else doesn't look the way I imagined transvestites. She is sophisticated and elegant, but her appearance has nothing of the exaggerated femininity of some of the showgirls here. I examine her for a long time, realise that I'm staring and then turn back to Samuel, embarrassed.

He raises his glass to me; everyone is talking at the same time and laughing. Maria comes into her own in this setting: her ironic wit makes much more sense here than at the sober Bauhaus. She and Else huddle together and gossip, while I needle Samuel with questions. At some point, he says, Herrliberg was too confining for him: he wanted to see more of the world. The first few months he spent in Berlin were hard. An older man put him up for a while but did not have the best of intentions. Shortly afterwards, Samuel contracted syphilis.

'If I hadn't heard of the Hirschfeld Institute, I would have died,' says Samuel. I'm surprised by his openness, but on the other hand, he always was a hypochondriac, and never had difficulty talking about his illnesses in detail. Why should it be any different with a venereal disease? He describes his life at the institute at length. 'I found my family there. No one considered it strange that I was attracted to men.' So I was right, after all. It had occurred to me in Weimar already that Samuel had also fallen in love with Jakob.

I want to hear more about the institute, but Else and Maria pull us on to the dance floor. A man in a tailcoat is singing on stage, making theatrical gestures in the direction of his all-women band. It seems to be a famous song because everyone dancing joins in for the chorus, practically drowning out the singer. The lyrics resound all around me:

We're not afraid to be queer and different
if that means hell – well, hell we'll take the chance
they're all so straight, uptight, upright and rigid
they march in lockstep we prefer to dance

Tall Else takes my hand and whirls me around in a circle until I'm dizzy. 'Lavender nights are our greatest treasure, where we can be just who we want to be!' Samuel booms in my direction. There is pride in his voice; and I think, Why not? Why not be proud, why not live together without marriage, why not love whoever you want, however you want?

The rest of the evening passes in a frenzy, and I lose all sense of time. I dance with Maria, Else, Samuel, and finally in between two tall transvestites. The mood of abandon no longer feels threatening but is liberating, like an embrace. Everything glows and spins. I'm breathless, I stop thinking, I forget to drink, I let myself be spun around, I let myself go.

～

The next morning, I wake up much too early. The whole flat rattles with the sound of banging doors and clattering cutlery. In my nightdress, I shuffle down to the parlour. My mother is tidying up, pauses for a moment when I enter and glares at me.

'So, Madame has risen, has she? This came for you,' she says, passing me a folded triangular piece of paper.

In accurate handwriting, it says:

Dear Luise, sorry that I haven't replied sooner. Sending telegrams has become too dangerous. I'll be at the Hellmuth on Görlitzer Straße from 4 p.m. today and will wait for you there.
Yours, Friedrich.

I look up from the letter into my mother's eyes.

'Do you think I don't notice that you're spending the nights gallivanting around? Who knows what kind of riffraff you're consorting with! The boy who brought the note did not make a good impression, that's for sure. What will the neighbours think? You know that the Görlitzer Bahnhof area is a writhing pit of Bolsheviks. Are you a communist now?'

'Was Friedrich here? Did he have red hair?' I ask.

'No, he didn't, but that's beside the point. I've had enough. Behave like a decent young lady for as long as you're living under my roof. If Otto were here, he would have—'

Otto! Always the mighty Otto. I'm about to hurl back at her that the 'riffraff' she is so scared of are worth a hundred times more than the 'decent people' she knows. But instead, I feel dangerously calm. It is pointless. Slowly, I leave the room, pack my suitcase with trembling hands, give Lore a brief hug, and leave my parents' house for the last time. Gradually I calm down and set my luggage on the ground. Four o'clock is a long way off, so there's no point in setting off for Kreuzberg already. In a situation like this in the past, I would have asked Charlotte to put me up, but she's in New York and judging from her last letter, there's no reason to expect her back any time soon. I know that Maria and Samuel are staying somewhere in Tiergarten, but I don't know their address.

I wander down Niebuhrstraße, where a hairdressing salon catches my eye. Since last summer, I have been toying with the idea of getting a bowl cut, now very fashionable at the Bauhaus, following the style of a Japanese painter in Paris. The only thing that always stopped me was the thought of my mother's reaction. But that no longer matters, I think, with a stony smile, as I enter the salon. A haircut costs one mark. All I have in my pocket is a five-mark note and my return ticket to Dessau. But nothing in the world seems more important to me right now than losing my old-fashioned, ladylike haircut. I watch in the mirror as my thick, stubborn curls fall away, giving me a great sense of satisfaction.

On the way to Görlitzer Bahnhof, I stare at myself, this now unfamiliar person, in every window I pass. Once I leave the underground, I walk down lively Wiener Straße. To get to Görlitzer Straße, I have to circumvent the enormous railway station. The fenced-off tracks stretch out into the distance. The area is dirtier than Charlottenburg, where my mother lives – all the houses are blackened with soot. An apparently endless grey swathe of clouds hovers in the sky. The Hellmuth bar is on the corner. Two sombre-looking men sit out front. I feel very out of place, but I want to see

Friedrich. I want him to know that his old friends haven't abandoned him.

The shorter of the two men blocks my way. Stammering, I manage to say that I'm an old friend of Friedrich's, causing him to stand to one side. 'Back room,' the taller one says gruffly.

It's smoky in the bar. Small clusters of young people hardly older than twenty sit around enormous wooden tables. Large letters on the wall pronounce, *The Red Front lives!* A group in the corner takes note of me, they whistle and laugh. I pass them by quickly, enter the back room via a swinging door with frosted glass, and see Friedrich sitting with other men at a table, bent over a map. He's given up on the pomade, it seems: his hair is as tousled and unkempt as it was in Weimar. When he spots me, he shoos the other men to one side and gives me a hasty, stiff hug.

He looks worn out and weary, but also euphoric. His eyes shining, he tells me about the battles they fight every day, and about the idealistic young people who have organised themselves into wild gangs and taken up arms against the Hitler Youth and the Steel Helmets' league. On Wiener Straße, he says, there is a pub where the SA meet up, and his friends are planning an attack.

'So you don't do anything but bash each other's heads in? What good will that do?'

'The war on the streets is at least as important as the party struggle. Luise, the Steel Helmets, the vigilantes, the SA – they're all dangerous. They harass innocent pedestrians! We can't just stand by and let that happen! The police don't do anything about it.'

'What about your architecture studies? You're wasting your talent here.'

'That way of thinking is so narrow-minded! But that's what you're like, all of you, sitting in Dessau and making your art works for the bourgeoisie. You don't even realise that people elsewhere are fighting for our future.'

I don't want to argue with him. I tell Friedrich about my precarious situation since fighting with my mother, but I keep it short. No matter how annoyed I am with her, I don't want to be a target of ridicule with my rich people's problems.

'I'm afraid you can't stay with me, Luise. I don't have any permanent place to live myself. I crash at comrades' flats, and when I can't find a place to stay, I sleep here.'

'Maria and Samuel are staying in that institute, I think – the Hirschfeld Institute?'

'The Hirschfeld Institute, interesting. So, Samuel has joined the queer brigade.' He gives his throaty chuckle for the first time since our reunion. 'If you want, I can find out where it is.'

Friedrich waves over one of the men who have retreated into the corner of the room. He seems to have a position of authority here: the man immediately goes away and returns with a large, dog-eared city map. It's hard for me to leave Friedrich again. I'm worried about him, but at the same time, I can't relate to what he's doing. 'Take care of yourself,' I say as I leave, but he has already turned back to his map.

~

Samuel, Maria and I are sitting and chatting on the green velvet sofa in the library when someone cries for help at the entrance. We rush to the door and find two boys standing there. One has his arm around the other to prop him up. His right eye is swollen, blood gushing from his nose and mouth. He looks terrible. We're not the only ones who have heard the cries for help: a good twenty people from the institute gather around the pair. An older woman in an apron says, 'Come on in, for a start,' lifts up the injured boy and leads him into the living room. We form an odd procession: at the front, the injured boy, who is half-dragged, half-carried along, and behind him, men in ballroom dresses, sailor's hats and formal suits. Also: women in formal suits, low-cut dresses and boyish workers' trousers. And bringing up the rear, there's Samuel who is still wearing lipstick, slender Maria and me with my bowl cut.

The boy is carefully laid on a pink sofa. 'I'll fetch Magnus,' says Samuel and disappears. Soon, he comes back with the man who was introduced to me yesterday evening as 'Auntie Magnesia', and who runs the institute. He bends over the patient, which causes his small spectacles to slip down his nose. As his large moustache trembles and he dabs the boy's nose carefully, he shakes his head.

'Those Hitler thugs again?' he asks.

The boy's friend answers: 'Hard to say. They weren't wearing armbands. But the way they lashed out at us made them seem like SA people. We were lucky – there were some people around. Why do you always have to answer back, Hans?'

The boy on the sofa lifts his head and hisses angrily, 'I'm

not going to let those hoodlums insult me!' Then he groans and sinks back on to the cushion.

'Nothing seems to be broken,' says Hirschfeld, straightening up. 'You're lucky, but be more careful in the future. Let's drink a schnapps to calm our nerves.'

Everyone seems relieved, at least for the moment. The woman in the apron, who I guess is the housekeeper here, disappears briefly and returns with a large tray of schnapps glasses. Half an hour later, we are all scattered around the room on the floor, or in the large winged armchairs and sofas, talking and laughing. Hans holds an ice compress to his cheek and enjoys the attention from Hirschfeld, who keeps looking over at him in concern, his brow deeply furrowed. A woman has sat down next to me who introduces herself as Helene Stöcker, immediately wanting to be on first-name terms. She is plump, has an ample bosom and is wearing a loose-fitting dress and an exotic scarf. Helene starts quizzing me in a way no one has done for a long time. She is particularly interested in my housing estate project. I readily explain my plans to her, sometimes losing myself in specialist terminology, and notice for the first time how much I have learned over the past year and how well I've thought my project through. When she asks me how likely it is that my plans will be realised, I tell her about my wretched presentation, my brief talk with Meyer and my doubts. It does me good to have someone listen and take me seriously.

'You shouldn't let all that put you off,' says Helene. 'You know, men don't like it when women trespass on their territory. And architecture, in particular, is an area that men think they have a special claim on – they can't even imagine women building houses!'

'Yes, well, perhaps I'm just not talented enough ...'

'Please, Luise, don't let them tell you that. You sound anything but incompetent. You know, this Meyer guy might not even mean to be nasty. It's just that in his view, mathematics, statics and construction are a male domain, which you can't even begin to understand. And when you do understand, they might find it threatening, like Karl, that student you mentioned. He wants to belittle you because you're a woman. Isn't there anyone else who might be able to help you other than this Meyer?'

I consider her suggestion for a moment. Gropius is only in Dessau occasionally these days, but he at least has always listened to me. During our last conversation, I even got the feeling he respected me, that we talked almost as equals. I decide to discuss my project with him. If I want to make progress, I need help.

I am impressed by Helene's energy and confidence. She talks about her political work, her commitment to peace, and her women's group that is fighting for abortion rights. I think of Friedrich, and for a moment, I have the feeling that our work at the Bauhaus is shamefully removed from any real political struggle. Helene talks about the evolution of the race, which would be possible with better birth control, and she suddenly sounds like Itten. I look over at Samuel who is sitting on the lap of a woman in a suit and is caught up in a lively discussion with Maria.

After dinner together at a long table, a small theatre performance takes place in the living room. It's a comedy featuring a heavily made-up inspector and his minion who are trying to solve the murder of a civil servant. There isn't much plot, but they make up for this with spells of singing and dancing.

Maria and I sleep in Samuel's room. He has built a fort for us of blankets and pillows, and soon the three of us are lying in the dark, whispering. I ask Samuel about Itten's followers, but all I find out is that Johannes has founded his own school in Berlin. He doesn't know whether Sidonie, Jakob and Erich are also in town. He seems to find it painful talking about his old friends, so I change the subject and ask him about his new life here at the institute, which he talks about gladly and at length. He speaks of Magnus Hirschfeld with the greatest respect and very fondly of his friends, who all support each other. I am happy that shy Samuel has found his place in life, and that someone is looking after him for a change. It is dawn before we sleep.

~

Hermann has a lot to say about my 'wild weekend in Berlin', and even more to say about my new haircut. I know he means it humorously, but I can sense his jealousy. It doesn't bother me. On the contrary, I find it touching that he is so obvious about it. Besides, he is right somehow. I might not have had a wild affair, but when I saw him after my weekend away, it felt as if I had been gone for a very long time. I can't forget what Helene Stöcker said about my work. I want to revise my plans for the housing estate one last time and then show them to Gropius. He will understand what I have in mind. I often see Miss Schild, who has become much friendlier towards me because of my job as a Bauhaus guide. She gives me one of the director's sought-after free appointments.

I sit at Hermann's table and try to concentrate. Hermann is lying on the bed reading, but he interrupts me every two minutes to tell me what he has just read. It annoys me, but at the same time, I am not disciplined enough not to be distracted. He talks at length about his commission for the Suchard advert and how he managed to kick out a colleague by writing a resignation letter in his name, which seems completely crazy to me. 'Haven't you gone a little too far?' I ask. He shakes his head in amusement.

'You're starting to scare me, Hermann.'

'Oh come on, these are just strategies. You need them to get ahead in life.'

I wonder how he manages to achieve anything at all. He always has a thousand things on his mind, and he's always meeting new people, going to exhibitions and writing letters. The only thing I never see him do is to work quietly. He scrambles up, strolls over to the table, takes the pen out of my hand and kisses me insistently. I protest half-heartedly. 'My diligent little Luise! You have the whole morning tomorrow!' I give up and let him carry me over to the bed. We sleep together, but it feels a little humdrum, a little too familiar. I think of Jakob and miss his intensity. But when I get up afterwards and carry out my douche, I feel grateful: it's precisely at moments like these when Hermann's experience with women shows. He has none of Jakob's shamefaced naïvety when it comes to this side of our love.

Hermann wakes me before it's even bright outside. He has

turned on the light, is in his bathrobe and holds out a cup of coffee. I groan and hide my head under the pillow, but he pulls it away again immediately. 'Come on, chin up! If you get up now, you can still get quite a bit done before your meeting,' he says. Dead tired, I sit down at the desk. When he comes back from his shower, he tells me about a student from László Moholy-Nagy's photography course who is looking for male and female models to work with today.

'You know I have to prepare for my meeting,' I say.

'Well, then I'll go and ask Maria,' he says, a comeback that I find so childish that I don't even bother to answer.

'Have fun,' is all I say, impatient to hear the door close behind him.

I read and do various calculations for a few hours, then I hastily pack my things and set off to meet Gropius. The way Hermann does things just for the sake of doing them has eaten up a lot of my time, and I'm annoyed that he doesn't seem to take my work seriously enough to leave me in peace. Ilse Schild gives me one of her rare friendly looks and, for the second time this year, I enter the director's office. Gropius is carefully sorting out papers on his desk. Without looking up, he says, 'Miss Schilling, I'm afraid I don't have a great deal of time. But please, take off your coat and sit down.' I do as he asks. Then he looks up and smiles. 'How are you getting on in the architecture department?' My nervousness causes my head to pound. I quickly explain that I have not come because of the architecture department, pull my plans out of my bag and spread them out in front of him. 'Ah, your housing estate! Let me have a look.' Gropius seems genuinely interested, which comes as a complete surprise after my experience with Meyer.

He is particularly taken by the way the buildings are aligned, and studies this for a long time. I explain in detail what considerations played a role in my decisions, how I did my calculations, and why I think light and air are more important than the mere size of the living space. Gropius asks questions and makes suggestions for improvement. Many of them are useful, and I'm delighted that he's taking me seriously enough to want to improve my design. At the end of our talk, he encourages me to keep working on it. Before he can bring our conversation to an end, I screw up all my courage and ask him if he has heard of any competitions that I might be able to enter. At this point, it's clear that I have gone too far. Gropius' expression becomes dismissive, and he contracts his bushy eyebrows. 'Students have practically no chance in architectural competitions. But well, OK, I'll let you know if I hear anything.' He stands up, and I take this as my cue to leave.

Back in Hermann's room, I throw my portfolio into a corner and take a deep breath. All in all, it was a success, I think, and I pour myself a glass of flat prosecco left over from yesterday. I hear a noise in the corridor and then Maria and Hermann burst into the room giggling. Maria is wearing dark lipstick, and her head is covered in a silk scarf. I don't manage to tell them about my meeting because they are so wrapped up in their experience that they forget to ask me. 'Hermann had to put on so many silly hats – I have no idea where the photographer found them all!'

'True, I wonder where he found them. Luise, you

should have seen what Maria was wearing. She looked like a queen!'

'A queen? Queens don't wear turbans!' Maria says, but she is visibly flattered.

'Really, you looked like an African queen, a tribal leader!' That lewd expression appears again on his face.

The dynamic between them makes me uneasy. I have the feeling that the two of them are playing a game and the only rule is that I have already lost. I remain seated at the table and look at them both, the glass of warm bubbly in my hand. But it's not jealousy I feel; it's incredulousness that they enjoy making me feel bad. And I know that anything I might say would sound like just that – petty, annoying jealousy. So I struggle to keep calm and tell myself that I am probably overreacting. If they both knew how much they were hurting me, they would never treat me like this. Surely, that can't be their intention.

~

In our in-house amphitheatre there is going to be a performance of *The Weimar Affair* tonight. The Bauhaus opening in Dessau was exactly a year ago today – reason enough to commemorate its origins in Weimar. On top of that, it's Kandinsky's birthday. Just like last year, we sit squeezed together on the canteen stools, but this time I am surrounded by friends. I'm sitting on Hermann's lap, with Josua and Maria flanking us. The students on stage are hell-bent on getting as many laughs out of the audience as possible. Moholy-Nagy is played by a boy with a severe centre parting and round glasses, making wild gestures and hamming up his Hungarian accent. A handful of other students play the introductory course participants, nodding eagerly and deliberately misunderstanding the master's instructions: they are told to build a 'ladder of feelings', an exercise that Moholy-Nagy really carried out in the introductory course, and for this, they bring wool, wire and a broom on to the stage. They use these materials to build an actual ladder, eliciting laughs from the entire audience. When they finally fetch a sausage to crown their ladder, the audience goes completely wild and erupts into hoots, applause and shouting.

After the performance, we go and sit in the canteen and talk about this depiction of the Weimar period. Hermann criticises the play with his usual nonchalant scepticism, and Maria and I disagree, pretending to be outraged. The two of us, after all, are the only two at the table who were actually there. Hermann gives in and turns to the subject of the poster announcing the festival: 'That's what happens when you don't let the advertising department do the work, but leave it to Schlemmer and his theatre people. What a bunch of dilettantes! They have no idea what you can achieve with the right advertising!'

Josua laughs. 'What exactly do you want to achieve? That every Bauhaus student comes to the Bauhaus festival? That's not a big challenge.'

'I think one must take even the small projects seriously,' Hermann replies. 'It's going to take a while before I can organise large political campaigns and move the masses. And until that time comes, I am going to practise on you Bauhaus people. But now I'm going to fetch us all something to drink.' He kisses me, lifts me off his lap and stands up.

A long queue has formed at the drinks counter, and Maria, Josua and I all watch Hermann push his way through to the front before turning around and waving at us. 'Move the masses, what utter nonsense,' says Josua, laughing.

'To be honest, I'm starting to find his delusions of grandeur creepy,' I say. 'He gets up in the middle of the night because he's had some brainwave, then walks around the room making notes and holding lectures. He only ever gets about two hours' sleep a night. Has he always been like that?'

'It comes and goes in phases. Sometimes he hides away in his room for months. I prefer the state he's in right now,' says Josua.

'I'm not sure. It worries me. And I don't like the way he talks to some people. He can be very domineering,' I say.

'Oh, come one, Lu, don't always start moralising,' says Maria. 'We all do what we want here. If we started setting up rules all over the place, things wouldn't be half as fun.'

'But without any rules, nothing works, does it?'

'Good old Luise,' says Josua, 'she's always worrying.' And the pair of them laugh at me lovingly.

'Don't worry, my child, especially as far as Hermann is concerned. I think his exuberance might well have something to do with you.'

I manage a smile. Maria is right in a way. Our lack of rules and acceptance of each other's quirks and idiosyncrasies make me feel comfortable in this group. Perhaps my father's principles have influenced me more than I realised.

Hermann has returned and plonks a bottle of wine on the table. We change the subject. Hermann doesn't notice; he wants to talk about the Poelzig Festival in February. Hans Poelzig is a lecturer at the Technical University of Berlin and has invited all the Bauhaus students to a costume party. We make plans: I can no longer stay with my mother, and it won't be possible for the three of us to sleep at the Hirschfeld Institute.

Hermann says: 'Luise, didn't you mention that Friedrich sometimes sleeps in the bar where you met him? What's it called again . . . ?'

'The Hellmuth. But believe me, you don't want to sleep there. It's scary. Even Friedrich said it was dangerous.'

'Don't worry, I'll look after you both,' says Hermann and puts an arm around Maria, which feels to me like a punch in the gut.

'That's not a bad idea,' says Maria. I throw her a warning glance, but she doesn't seem to understand.

'It's a dive bar! It doesn't even have beds!' Now I feel desperate.

'Oh, come on, Luise, it'll be an adventure! Maria, what do you say?'

'Yay, an adventure!' shouts Maria.

'How do you even know that Friedrich wants to see you? You haven't talked to him in ages,' I object.

'Friendships aren't over that easily.' Hermann says this with great indifference.

'An adventure!' Maria shouts again. Their silliness aggravates me. But there's no point. I have little choice but to give in and hope that it all turns out well.

Now the chairs and tables are pushed aside, and the Bauhaus choir takes up position in front of the windows. Josua leads Maria on to the dancefloor with a spring in his step, and the other students at our table also stand up. Hermann starts nuzzling my neck, but I pull away, trying as diplomatically as possible to explain my concerns about his change in behaviour. To my relief, he isn't even annoyed and doesn't try to deny anything at all. He shrugs and says: 'It's just a feeling of elation that comes from being so madly in love with you.' The idea that I could have such a huge effect on his mood is so flattering that I feel warm inside. I nestle up to him and say nothing. Closely entwined, we watch the others on the dancefloor, enjoying the sight of Josua whirling Maria so fast that she almost loses her balance. I think of Christmas approaching and feel grateful all of a sudden to have my substitute family here, who make me feel so snug and secure.

~

An acrid smell of turpentine stings my nose, pulling me out of my deep sleep. It takes a couple of minutes for me to find my bearings. Outside it is gloomy; Hermann has turned on the ceiling light and is bending over the limestone he dragged up to his room a few days earlier from the printing workshop. Now I understand where the stench is coming from: he is working on a lithograph. It is going to be part of a collage that is growing bigger and bigger, already taking up half the wall. With trembling hands, I reach for Hermann's silver watch that is lying on the bedside table. It's two o'clock in the afternoon. My mouth is dry, my nose blocked and when I sit up, my head spins. Snatches of the night before filter through to me as if over a long distance: Hermann almost lovingly spacing out the white powder a friend brought from Berlin on the table; Josua, urging us to be good Christians and to sing a few Christmas carols; Maria sitting on the balcony, shouting pointless slogans into the night. And then, me again: talking to Bayer, convincing him that I'm the most talented architect that the Bauhaus has ever seen; on the dancefloor in the foyer at the official Christmas party, my arms flapping; having an intense discussion with Hermann in which we plan our meteoric rise; excitedly following Maria's secret sign to retreat back to Hermann's room. The embarrassment makes my stomach contract. There was cocaine sometimes at Charlotte's parties, but it wasn't until last night, when the secrecy of it turned us into conspirators, that I was tempted to try it myself.

I close my eyes and try to bury my recollections in sleep. But I can't: my heart is racing, and I feel cold. I concentrate on my breathing. The techniques I learned in Weimar have often kept me in good stead. But this time, breathing doesn't make me calmer – it does the opposite, in fact, and there seems to be something stuck in my throat. It blocks my breathing, making me feel like I'm falling down an endless hole. Hermann has noticed that I'm awake. I try to show how panicked I am, my face red, unable to speak because I can't breathe. He sits down on the edge of the bed, first trying to soothe me with a hug and glass of water. When this doesn't help, he grabs a paper bag and signals that I should breathe in and out of it. Slowly, my throat relaxes, and I calm down. We sit there, dazed and panting, until we finally burst out laughing in relief.

~

The large spots of light on the station floor in Anhalter Bahnhof make me feel sad. When I was little, my mother would sometimes pick up my father from this station, and to pass the time while we were waiting for him to arrive, my mother would use these light spots as prompts to tell me stories from the New Testament – 'God's rays', she would call them. Although my life couldn't be further away from my parents' dry piety, I think back wistfully to those moments. I haven't heard a word from my mother in months, and at the moment, I'm not sure that we'll ever be reconciled.

Maria and Hermann are caught up in the kind of fever-ish anticipation that only a huge party can bring. I push my gloomy thoughts aside and let their enthusiasm infect me. The three of us are trudging through the snow, arms linked, with me in the middle. Poelzig's party is taking place at the Technical University in Charlottenburg; we have a few hours to spare and are on our way to the Flechtheim Gallery on Lützowufer where Professor Klee's pictures are currently being exhibited. I have never seen his paintings on display, only occasional works-in-progress. I spend a long time in the gallery, plunging into the colourful picture puzzles – a collection of human machines, strange animals and plants and fantastic objects. In the catalogue, a famous surrealist author writes: 'Good morning, little creature with the endless gaze, algae without rocks, thank you, beings, vegetations, things which do not support the common ground ... ' I don't manage to read on because Hermann discovers the bar and drags me there. I am deeply impressed and once again proud to study at a university where artists of Klee's calibre teach, even attracting admiration from the surrealists in Paris. I want to share my feelings with the other two, but they are so engrossed in their witty banter that I don't even try. Finally, I lead them through Tiergarten and take a detour to Savignyplatz. We watch and comment on the passers-by, stare into brightly lit shop windows and start a snowball fight that soon peters out. Hermann invites Maria and me to drink a hot chocolate and then have an extravagant dinner. We're all in a lively mood but it takes every ounce of my energy to keep up with them: the conversation races back and forth, new insider jokes are constantly being cracked, plans are made and just as quickly aborted.

In the past few weeks, there have been an abundance of occasions for wild parties at the Bauhaus. After the Christmas revelries, there were countless evenings spent at Hermann's in the Prellerhaus, then New Year's Eve, when we stood on the roof and gazed up at the sky, and finally, a couple of other bigger parties. Each time, Hermann insisted on staying until the end. I am so exhausted that my body seems to be subsisting on reserve energy, and so tired I can't even appreciate how tired I am. There's a gnawing feeling of guilt at the back of my mind: I have only half-finished one of my course projects and haven't even handed in another. But I also don't want to miss out on all the fun and extravagance – and if I'm honest, I don't want to leave Maria and Hermann alone together. It's as if I'm on a roundabout that keeps spinning faster, and if I lose concentration for a moment, I'll go flying.

I can still feel the effects of the bottle of champagne that Hermann ordered in a grand manner at dinner as we go through a side entrance to the university and enter a large hall. It is funny to see this many Bauhaus students in another city, all dressed in their striking costumes. We constantly stop and talk to people. Hermann introduces me to the few Dessau students that I don't know yet. He makes no secret about the fact that we're a couple: on the contrary, he is proud to have me at his side. The chairs have been pushed aside, the high ceilings have been hung with silver garlands, and in the darkened corners couples are lying on a few straw sacks in tight embrace. Dozens of bottles of wine and champagne are standing on the tables. I take a glass and drink to keep my fatigue at bay. It doesn't help much. The more I drink, the less I can stand the crowds around me. The sounds of conversations and music brew into an unbearable din, the dancers whirling about look like shot-putters hurtling out of control, and the lights hurt my eyes. I am suddenly desperate to get out of here, this very minute. I look around for Hermann. He is standing at a table, talking to Maria and the photographer who shot portraits of them both in Dessau.

I take Hermann aside. 'Can we leave?'

'What? Already? The party's only just starting!' He turns to Maria, clasps his forehead theatrically and shouts to her over the noise, 'Did you hear that? Luise wants to go to bed already!'

'No, Lu, we can't go yet! Please don't be a bore!' Maria shouts back.

The photographer pushes his way through to me and says, 'You're Luise, aren't you? I've heard so much about you. My name is Gustav.' I don't want to be impolite, so I start a conversation with this Gustav, who so badly wants to talk to me. Through the buzz of noise, I hear Hermann and Maria speaking in hushed tones right behind me. In a conspiratorial voice, Hermann says, 'That's good. He's distracting her; then we can stay a bit longer.'

'Yes, I hope he charms her. No one can resist Gustav.' They're talking about me the exact same way we talk about people we don't like. I feel humiliated for a moment, but then the anger takes over.

I turn around and say: 'You know, I can hear every word you're saying. Loud and clear. Stay, for all I care! I'm off!' I leave Gustav standing there as I thread my way through the crowd.

Hermann catches up with me at the entrance. He tries to placate me. 'You didn't want to spend the night at Friedrich's place anyway. Perhaps we can stay here and sleep on the straw sacks later on?' He seems not to have heard me when I said I wanted to leave! His insistence only makes me angrier.

'Do what you want! I'm sure Maria will share a straw sack with you.' When Hermann finally comprehends that I refuse to stay, he gives in. He glances ruefully around the room, gives me a grim smile, and accompanies me out.

Hermann hails a cab and I give the driver the address in a strained voice. We drive in silence through the brightly lit night until Hermann finally says: 'Luise, we have to talk about your jealousy. It just can't go on like this.' His accusation is so unfair and preposterous that I have no idea how to react.

'I'm not in the least jealous. It's just that you and Maria—'

'There you go again: Maria, Maria, Maria. Don't focus on

her so much.' The fact that he doesn't listen to me is bad enough, but his mocking tone makes me utterly incredulous.

'What kind of way is that to talk to me?'

Hermann gives the driver a couple of banknotes, we get out and stand in front of the pub. 'Friedrich still doesn't know that we want to sleep here, does he?' I ask.

'Don't worry; come on, it'll be an adventure.' I'm tired and angry, and the last thing I feel like is an adventure. We go into the Hellmuth. The pub's main room is in semi-darkness, with just four men playing cards at a table. When Hermann asks if Friedrich is here, they shake their heads mutely. Hermann doesn't skip a beat: he lays a hand across my shoulders, claims we are comrades, members of the Communist Party from Dessau, and that we need a place to stay for the night. Astonishingly, it seems to work. One of the men stands up bad-temperedly and guides us up a narrow staircase to the first floor. In a small room that doubles as a storage space, several straw sacks are wedged between a jumble of clothes, posters, books and boxes. The man wishes us goodnight and disappears.

I look around feeling wretched and wondering what I am doing here in the first place. 'I don't want to sleep here, Hermann,' I say.

'Just a minute ago, you wanted to leave the party come what may, and now you don't want to be here. There's just no pleasing you,' he says, rolling his eyes.

We start to argue: our first real fight. We argue about the room we're in, about Maria, about my supposed jealousy. His expression remains fixed; he looks at me as if I were a nuisance. He continues to talk to me in his patronising, scornful tone. I feel trapped in the situation, robbed of my freedom. Even if I could leave this dump, I can't think of anywhere to go. I get louder and louder, while Hermann stays deliberately calm. 'I just don't understand what this is all about, Luise.'

I try to express myself clearly, but at some point, I am so enraged that I stammer. Hermann watches me, his arms crossed behind his head, then suddenly he imitates me, stuttering and grasping for words. And then he starts laughing, deriding me. There's a buzzing in my head. What is going on here? I step in his direction, he carries on laughing, and then for some reason, he says: 'If you weren't such a little weakling, you'd hit me now.' For a split second, I'm surprised at his invitation, then I raise my hand and slap him across the face.

A searing pain shoots through my nose into my head. It's as if time has unravelled. I reach up to touch my nose, then stare at my bloody fingers and start to slowly comprehend that the fist that just came hurtling towards my face was meant for me, and that it was Hermann's. I stare at him, aghast. He has stopped laughing but seems unmoved that he has injured me. 'Don't be surprised if I hit back,' he says.

Now I am gripped by naked fear. If someone who loved me just a minute ago, someone I trust, can hurt me so badly and not show any remorse, who knows what else could happen? 'Look what you've done,' I say, wiping my hand across my face. I realise that I'm crying. My words are an appeal to a shared reality, a world in which the weaker do not get hit and this was all a big mistake – one Hermann deeply regrets.

'Don't be so dramatic,' he says drily. I know that he is stronger than me, but I use up my last energy anyway by punching his arm, perhaps to prove that I can defend myself and that he can't beat me to death in this secluded room. He doesn't even flinch. All my strength drains away and I feel weak and exhausted. Hermann turns his back on me and pays me no attention whatsoever. With all the calm in the world, he takes off his expensive suit and lies down on one of the straw sacks. I drag the other to the furthest corner of the room, then my body finally collapses. I lie down, cradle my head in my arms and cry myself to sleep.

Loud noises wake me up, and I try lifting my heavy head. I can't breathe through my nose, it's swollen, and my temples are throbbing. Hermann is up, hastily dressing. He considers me with a cursory glance. 'I'm going to catch the train home. Are you coming?' he finally asks when he is already standing at the door. The decision overwhelms me; I can't make sense of last night's events. I was planning to visit Samuel today. But I feel sick at the thought of having to explain my injured nose to him. So I drag myself to my feet, straighten out my dress and follow Hermann downstairs in silence.

We board the train at Görlitzer Bahnhof. I stare out at the grey city passing us by. Thinking of last night, I feel a burning shame for getting myself into a situation where things could get so out of control. To be hit by a man in the shabby attic of a communist bar isn't a story that fits into my life. I look over at Hermann who is hiding behind a newspaper. It's confusing to still have such strong feelings for him. I desperately want to reverse last night's events. But I don't know how.

'Should we talk?' I eventually ask.

Hermann lowers his newspaper and looks at me impassively. It seems he has been waiting for me to ask. 'I have never seen anyone lose their mind like you did last night, Luise. I truly have no idea what it is about me that makes you act so crazy.'

I don't want to accept this explanation of last night's events, but at the same time, I want to go back to our easy, familiar manner. Most of all, I want him to look at me with that thrilled, enamoured gaze again, to which I have become so accustomed. Who knows, perhaps I am to blame for the way things turned out last night. Again, I run through the events, looking for something for which I can apologise. In the end, I say: 'I shouldn't have put pressure on you to leave the party. I'm sorry.' But this doesn't have the desired effect. Hermann grunts and turns back to his newspaper. We spend the rest of the journey in silence.

At Dessau station, I want to go home straight away. I set off in the direction of my flat, but Hermann says: 'Come over to mine, Josua and I want to make some food later on.' I touch my throbbing nose gingerly. I can't believe that Hermann wants to return to normality so quickly.

As gently as possible, I say: 'I have to straighten myself out first. Let's talk tomorrow.'

He nods gravely and says: 'That's good. You should figure out what was the matter with you.'

It takes me a while to get home. I stop at every crossing and have to persuade myself to carry on. The lorries and cars driving past seem menacing. My body is constantly expecting a collision.

~

The next day, I don't wake up until the early afternoon. I get up, pull open the curtains and lie back down again. I stare inertly into the darkness.

I pick over my feelings with an almost scientific interest: my helplessness, humiliation and my physical reactions. I realise how inexperienced I am. I have no idea what it is like to hit someone or to be hit. To be sure, there was evidence of violence everywhere after the war – on the streets, in the bars, on the tram. It was palpable; you could almost smell it; you could see it in the faces of some passers-by. For the first time, I realise how privileged I am that I never had to fear for my safety, that violence was always something that occurred elsewhere.

And Hermann gave me just that: a feeling of safety. He couldn't wish harm on me. He loves me. Maybe it is my fault, after all? But no matter: a relationship cannot survive something like this. It is an appalling thought, but I keep circling back to it.

Evening falls before I finally get up. I slowly dress, then sit down at the small table in the corner, write a letter and address it to Charlotte in New York. As clearly as I can, I explain what happened and ask her for advice. As I'm writing it all down, it becomes very clear: I have to break up with Hermann. To prevent myself from changing my mind, I also write that in the letter. My mouth is dry, and my head still hurts, but it helps to get everything down on paper. In the meantime, I am ravenous. I don't want to go the canteen because I don't want to run into anyone. In the end, I go to the pub where I worked last year. I'm in luck: the owner isn't there, and my former workmates look after me. No one asks about my swollen nose and black eye. Instead, they sit me down on a chair in the kitchen, lay a wool cover over my shoulders, and fetch me a bowl of soup.

I spend three days in my flat, staring at the ceiling and eating the bread and sausage that my old colleagues gave me to take home. Then I pull myself together, pick up an empty suitcase and go over to the Prellerhaus. I stand listening in front of Hermann's door for a while. He's at home; I can hear him bustling about in his room. I'm nervous but resolute, hold the suitcase like a protective shield in front of me and open the door. Hermann is tidying things in the same brisk way as ever, and he isn't at all surprised to see me. He acknowledges me with a curt greeting and a sober look. Then he sets down a cup of coffee for me and points wordlessly to the other chair. I sit down, somewhat reluctantly. The conversation that follows is an analysis of my mind: I am too ambitious, says Hermann, and put myself under too much pressure. I bite my lip. Instead of disagreeing, I say: 'That may all be true, Hermann. But we have to break up all the same.' I see something like respect surface in his eyes for a second, then I stand and pack my books, clothes and drawings.

When I've finished and am about to leave, Hermann says: 'So long, then.'

My body stiffens when he embraces me. Then I'm outside the door again and am surprised at how little time it took.

I run into Maria in the canteen. It is lunchtime, and there are hardly any spaces left at the long tables. The rattling of cutlery and murmuring of voices merge into a swell of industriousness. The snow outside in the courtyard steeps the room in a dazzling white. I feel exposed and vulnerable. Involuntarily, I touch my nose. It still hurts, but the injury is almost invisible now, as I assured myself this morning in the mirror. The swelling under my eye has also disappeared. Maria and I talk about all sorts of things while standing in line for lunch. When we finally sit down on two stools near the large windows, I try to tell her what happened after Poelzig's party in Berlin. She listens to everything, but her expression is remote, and I sense that she's not hearing this for the first time. Her large eyes have an almost faraway look. She says, 'No hard feelings, Luise, but I'd rather not take sides.' I feel very alone all of a sudden. Maria is my only friend here, and I had hoped for a little more loyalty. I eat as quickly as possible, then get up abruptly and say goodbye.

~

I urgently need to distract myself, but I can't work in my murky room. The library is a safe choice: Hermann has never ended up there, not even accidentally. From a distance, I spot him at the main entrance to the Bauhaus and have to repress my reflex to flee. I will not let myself be scared away from my own university. So I march purposefully through the frozen mud towards the building. On closer inspection, the person I thought was Hermann is, in fact, the foppish Herbert Bayer, whom I greet with a trembling hand. The small library room is empty and unheated, as always. I keep my coat on, turn up the radiator and sit down next to it on the floor. For the first time in a long while, I look at

my housing estate plans. In the months of partying before
going away to Berlin, I often did the bare minimum to pass
the course requirements. My few attempts at working were
always marred by feeling rushed and preoccupied. Now a
feeling of calm comes over me that I haven't felt in a long
time. I am happy that my concentration has returned – and
it is high time, too. In April, I have to present my work,
and hopefully receive my degree. Many of my fellow students have already secured jobs – Josua wants to go back to
Palestine and Karl has a position in Munich. I have nothing
but my housing estate plans. I decide to use the coming
month to think through Gropius' suggestions and construct
a model of two of the buildings.

I spend the next few hours by the gurgling radiator doing
revisions; then I stow away my portfolio. In the stairwell,
I run in to Josua, who is talking excitedly to Gustav, the
photographer. The two of them greet me amiably as if nothing at all has happened. Gustav invites Josua and me to see
his darkroom: he says his photos are ready and hanging up
to dry. We cross the connecting bridge to the photography
department, which I never had much to do with. Here,
Moholy-Nagy's students experiment with angles, perspective
and the geometry of technology. Pictures with shifted views
hang on the walls; objects crowd into the foreground, people
are blurred by shortened depth of field or reveal just one eye.
Soon we are looking in the semi-darkness of the darkroom
at Gustav's prints, which are hanging up to dry on a line. My
heart sinks when I recognise Maria and Hermann in one of his
photos. There isn't much to see, as they are both hidden by
an enormous globe that reflects the window. I try not to stare

too obviously at the photo. Josua's attention is elsewhere. He has spotted himself in one of the photographs and is asking Gustav about Moholy-Nagy's teaching methods.

'I have to decide what to do when Gropius leaves,' he says.

I prick up my ears. 'What do you mean?' I ask.

'Have you been living on another planet?' Josua asks. 'That's all anyone's talking about!'

I look at him cluelessly. Gustav and Josua quickly fill me in on what they know about the latest developments. They tell rumours of 'huge conflicts', of construction mistakes in the Törten Estate and its hugely dissatisfied residents. Gustav says that Gropius has announced his resignation for 1 April. Meyer will be taking over the directorship, and it is not sure whether Moholy-Nagy is staying either.

'If Moholy goes, I'm going too,' says Gustav.

'Perhaps it's just an April Fool's prank,' says Josua, and giggles at his own bad joke.

I'm just as unaffected as Josua by the news: if all goes well, I'll have my degree by April. But I'm shocked all the same – the director who built up everything here, asserting his vision over the years, is now handing over to Meyer, just because a few residents have complained about badly designed windows?

Josua shrugs. 'Gropius was hardly ever in Dessau and never visited the estate to listen to the complaints. As soon as he finishes a building, he loses interest. And that's not the only reason he's leaving. He was here so seldom in recent months that he wasn't really doing his job as director. But we don't have to worry about all that. We've almost finished!'

Gustav nods. 'You're lucky. But we'll give you a good

send-off, of course! Didn't Hermann want to throw a big farewell party?'

'Yes . . .' says Josua, embarrassed, before adding hastily: 'I don't know what happened between you two, but perhaps you'll have made up by then?'

I have no idea where I find the courage – perhaps simply because we are sitting in the dark – but I say: 'I'll tell you what happened.'

When I am finished, there is silence. Then Josua clears his throat and says: 'You should talk to Teddy. I think she left for Berlin before you came to Dessau. Hermann and Teddy were together for a while, and I think she would know what you're talking about.' I am baffled. I've never even heard of a woman called Teddy. So this is not the first time something like this has happened? How can Josua mention it so casually? I want to ask him, but he seems to find the subject unpleasant and gets up, saying: 'I'm hungry. Is anyone coming to the canteen?'

I shake my head. Gustav stares into the distance, seeming not to have heard the question. Then, very slowly, he looks up and declines. When Josua has left, he looks at me for a long time. 'Luise, I don't know if you want to talk to me, of all people, about this, because we hardly know each other. But what you've just told us . . . It's not OK!'

I'm astonished by his outrage.

'You have to go to the police!'

'But you can hardly see my injuries any more. I don't think the police will believe me,' I object. 'Apart from that, wouldn't that be going a bit too far? In the end, it was just a stupid argument.'

'It was violence! And against a woman, what's more – you don't hit people who are weaker than you! That's not what civilised people do, Luise.'

'But I provoked him . . .'

'Now, listen to me, it doesn't matter how much you provoked him. It's not your fault when someone hits you! And it seems that it wasn't the first time either. If you aren't prepared to go to the police, we should at least see to it that everybody finds out what kind of guy this Hermann is.'

I'm overwhelmed by Gustav's extreme reaction, so different to everyone else's. Everything he says sounds right to me. But the thought of telling even more people about the evening in Berlin scares me.

'What if no one believes me? What if they all think he left me and I was out for revenge?'

'That might happen. But what if you don't tell anyone and Hermann beats the next woman to death?'

The black-and-white photograph of Hermann and Maria, which I've been staring at this whole time, blurs before my eyes. The bitter smell of chemicals makes the room unbearably stuffy. All of a sudden, I feel exhausted.

~

Besides work, sleep is my only refuge from the thoughts reverberating in my head. I still wake up much too early every day – the images, pain, and my anger evicting me from my sanctuary. I lie in bed until dawn breaks and think about Hermann and me, Josua and Maria. After talking to Gustav, my foggy rage is now taking shape. I'm also angry at my friends. If Gustav is right, then why did Josua and Maria react as if nothing unusual had happened? And they're not the only ones. In the meantime, rumours about the night in Berlin have spread, but that hasn't stopped Hermann from sending out an endless stream of invitations for parties at the Prellerhaus. Since our weekend together, he is even more convivial than before. His name is on everyone's lips. His handmade posters, advertising the graduation party, hang from every wall. The people I wanted to build a new world with are turning into spineless hypocrites before my very eyes.

On the day of our final lecture, I force myself to use the time more usefully than just torturing myself with a never-ending loop of thoughts. As dawn breaks, I walk through the town's empty streets. It takes more than an hour from the Bauhaus to the Törten Estate. I want to know exactly what the residents feel is wrong with their housing. Maybe I will find out pitfalls to avoid in my own designs.

The Törten Estate was too far to include in my guided Bauhaus tours, and I haven't been here since my first days in Dessau. Although a patch of blue sky is showing for the first time in ages, everything seems too close together and deserted here. The residents must still be asleep; in any case, there is hardly anyone out on the streets. The square buildings span several streets, lined with window fronts. They look small under the utility poles towering above them. Two of the buildings I pass have been repainted and an elongated opening that is supposed to let in light on the stairwell through glass blocks has been bricked up. Finally, I pass a small front garden in which an elderly woman is kneeling and potting plants. I walk over to her and start a conversation. There is no need for me even to ask: as soon as we talk about the weather, she mentions the terrible insulation in the buildings. It is cold and draughty everywhere, she says; the steel window frames don't shut properly and the wind whistles through the gaps. At long last, she adds, they're going to start replacing the window frames with decent wooden ones.

I laugh on my way home. Gropius' sacred steel windows, replaced with vulgar wood. If the director only knew! On the other hand, nothing is stopping him from talking to the residents. I expect that steel window frames could be insulated too so that they could keep out the cold weather. I make a note to learn from this mistake. If I ever have the opportunity to realise a bigger project, I won't forget about it as soon as the next commission comes in.

For now, my last lecture of the semester is about to take place, the last event at which all students of the architecture department will assemble before the individual exams. Although the lecture doesn't start for another half-hour, crowds already fill the lecture hall. Even students from other departments have come because it is Hannes Meyer's first appearance since the announcement that Gropius is leaving the Bauhaus. Everyone is curious to see whether Meyer will comment on this. I see Josua standing with a group at the edge of a row of chairs. They are bending over something and having a lively discussion. After hesitating briefly, my curiosity gets the better of me, and I join them. Spread out in front of Josua is the blueprint of a construction plan. One of the students has smuggled it out of Gropius' office, Josua explains. Gropius has won the competition for an estate in Dammerstock near Karlsruhe. While everyone eagerly analyses the plan, I stare at the sheet of paper. Blood pounds in my temples and I go cold. I push my way nearer to the front and lean over the plan. There can be no doubt: these are almost exactly the same forms as on my housing estate plans. The basic idea of bar buildings and their narrowness, even their east-west alignment, is calculated in the same way. In a daze, I sit down on one of the chairs.

Meyer enters the room; the students quickly pack away their things and everyone sits down. My last lecture at the Bauhaus passes over my head. Initially, I feel outraged at my mentor's audacity; then I start to panic. In two days, I have to present my degree project, and I have spent all these months working solely on my housing estate. Gropius will no longer be here, but Meyer, Breuer and the other examining professors are certain to have already seen his Dammerstock plans. I cannot possibly show them anything other than my plans because there is no time to prepare anything. Meyer says a few closing words, trying his best at standard German, and applause cuts through to me from a long way off.

~

The presentations take place in the classroom. Every day, several students take their exam. Today is my turn – I am last. There is a commotion in the corridor. People make feverish last-minute changes; students scribble on their plans or practise their explanations. After the presentations, there are red faces and loud cheers; students storm out of the exam room holding their degree certificates aloft, are hugged or patted on the shoulder. Although there is a lot of compassion, it is not completely altruistic: those of us who have yet to sit our exams want to know what to expect. The other main topic of conversation is Hermann's party. I won't be going, of course. It pains me to think that all my fellow students will be celebrating their graduation and I can't be there.

Since my findings during Meyer's lecture, I haven't looked once at my plans. Even thinking about it makes my blood boil at the unfairness of the whole matter. I keep recalling details of my few conversations with Gropius in a dramatic, ominous way. Should I have guessed that he would help himself to my ideas when he advised me not to enter competitions? Did I behave unprofessionally? Should I never have shown him my plans?

In any case, it's too late for that now. Meyer opens the door and says: 'Miss Schilling, we're ready for you.'

Herbert Bayer is sitting in the room with Marcel Breuer, the designer of the steel-tubed chairs. Breuer is a young man with a gentle expression and a tweed suit; Bayer looks elegant and unapproachable as usual. I take my plans out of my portfolio, hang some of them up on the wall and spread out the rest before my small but distinguished audience. Step by step, sentence by sentence, I stumble through my presentation and try to forget Gropius, the Dammerstock estate and the competition. My explanations pick up pace, and I become livelier, satisfied by the usefulness of my project. I talk about fair distribution of air and light, about construction materials, and the use of green spaces. When I've finished, Bayer is the only one to ask me any questions. While I try to answer him in detail, I see Breuer and Meyer exchanging looks and showing each other their notes.

Then Meyer clears his throat and says: 'To be honest, Miss Schilling, we are wondering how a woman could come up with such a functional, not to say masculine, plan . . .'

I don't know what to say.

Breuer nods and says: 'We are very reluctant to doubt the integrity of a Bauhaus student. But your plans bear a striking resemblance to Walter Gropius' latest project. Would you like to comment on this, Miss Schilling?'

My worst nightmare has come true. I knew it would, I visualised it, still I'm in shock. My face feels like it's burning, my throat is tightening up, but there is no way out now. 'That's because I showed the director my plans a year back,' I say. 'It was unwise of me, but not deceitful.' I hear how defiant I sound and assume that it doesn't make me any more credible.

'Do you seriously mean to tell us all that an architect of Walter Gropius' standing and eminence would deem it necessary to steal ideas from a student?' Meyer asks indignantly.

Herbert Bayer looks troubled.

'I am sure there has been a misunderstanding,' says Breuer.

'But these are outrageous claims! We cannot simply let them go unchallenged!' Meyer says loudly.

'Gentlemen, please let's stay calm,' Breuer replies; and then, turning to me: 'These are serious allegations, Miss Schilling. Your plans are faultless, as you know. But in this case, we have to consult Mr Gropius.' I am told to wait in the room while the gentlemen try to reach Gropius by telephone. After a never-ending hour, they return.

'You're in luck, Miss Schilling,' says Meyer. 'Mr Gropius is more generously inclined than I would be in his situation. Naturally, he refutes your allegations, and you must be sure never to repeat such ridiculous claims. Gropius remembers you throughout your studies as a courageous and independent student. He values you. For that reason, we can award you your degree today. But, due to the similarity of your plans with Gropius', we will be forced to keep them here.'

I have difficulty speaking, but I see no alternative to swallowing this humiliation. Nodding, I hastily accept my diploma certificate and walk out in to the corridor. One student asks me how the exam went, then another asks whether I will be going to Hermann's party tonight. Wordlessly, I shake my head and carry on walking; I feel the tears coming, and the stairwell blurs in front of my eyes. I run the whole way to my flat and indiscriminately throw a few clothes and books into a suitcase. I leave my tools behind.

~

I stop on the railway platform.

I can see the Bauhaus from here. The afternoon sun shines on its walls, the glass façades lie in darkness. The building is no longer a gleaming white but has turned grey and dull. Lights are on in a few of the Prellerhaus windows, and the balconies line up in monotonous rows. The building stares at me. Right now, I am far away from the people inside who are sitting at the loom or in the canteen, arguing about the future or raising a glass in their rooms. Our aim was to make buildings for the New Man, someone affected and shaped by the new forms around him. But how can we ever achieve this if the new forms are being made by the same old people, with all their mistakes and flaws? A beam of light reflects in a window, dazzling me. I let my gaze pass over the gleaming façades one last time. Then I turn around and set off.

From Luise Schilling's estate

DIE ZEIT newspaper, 23 September 1965

Non-fiction title: recommendation of the month

Luise Schilling: *There Goes the Neighborhood: Social Enclaves in the Shadow of Urban Planning*, Sichter Verlag, Stuttgart. 368 pages, 12,80 DM

If you're interested in architecture, these days, chances are you're probably interested in the Bauhaus school. Such a proclivity will make this book by German-born American, Luise Schilling, who studied architecture at the Bauhaus before the war, all the more astounding. For her *There Goes The Neighborhood*, she makes a case against the kind of holistic city planning preached and practised at the Bauhaus. Instead, Schilling demands that the city is seen as it is: a cluster of small, independent economic zones and organic communities. According to the author's indignant thesis, urban planners are out of touch with urban populations. She argues that, however, it is the task of these planners to make cities habitable for people, rather than automobiles. For this to happen, Schilling says, they must prioritise pedestrian pavements and porches, the spaces that give a city life and make it safe, instead of building never-ending housing projects, skyscrapers and freeways.

Schilling studied under the famous Walter Gropius and emigrated to the United States in 1927. Today, the Bauhaus is regarded as one of the cradles of modernity, a utopian place. Although Schilling's book does not deride any particular vision, the question arises whether the author has turned her back on her mentors and is doing her part to subvert their worldview.

After all, the idea of controlled urban structuring began chiefly at the Bauhaus. The Bauhaus was the opposite of technophobic. Back then, it was considered only right to adapt the city to traffic. In her book, Schilling also dismisses the *unité d'habitation* – the type of living accommodation developed by the grand architectural master, Le Corbusier, as a means to offer cheap living space to masses of people – as 'quixotic nonsense'. Perhaps it was her brief employment at the New York Department of Buildings that inspired Luise Schilling to change her mind. In any case, by the end of the 1950s, she was already fighting against the construction of a freeway through the West Village, the New York district where she lived. Her initiative was surprisingly successful. The city withdrew its plans.

The book, which has been published for the first time in German translation, caused a stir in New York. In many places, Schilling's publication was dismissed as the writings of 'a militant housewife', whereas others venerated it as 'the salvation of the city by an outsider'. But this controversial book is worth reading not only because it polarises, but also because it is concise, illuminating and well written. We wait in suspense to hear the wake-up calls Miss Schilling broadcasts in the future.

KM

Return to sender – addressee not found

Luise Schilling
208 West 10th Street
NY 3

Maria Pfister
Zimmerlistr. 7
Zurich

New York, 16 September 1962

Dear Maria,

How happy I was to receive your letter! Of course I'm
not angry with Samuel for giving you my address. On
the contrary. He'd already told me, but it's good to read
for myself that you've survived these terrible, tumultuous
decades. It's strange somehow that so many of you
have ended up in Switzerland, the country that was

already a refuge for many of us in more peaceful times.
It comforts me to know that many of my old friends
have reunited. Tell me, how is Jakob? Is Sidonie still so
touchy? And Erich – did good, gentle Erich survive the
war years well?

Regarding the visit to Israel you suggested: I have to
see whether I can raise enough money to make such a
big trip. But I'm glad to hear that Josua is now making a
career as a politician there. Who'd have thought!

Sometimes I regret not saying goodbye before I left
Dessau. But there were reasons for that. I'll tell you
one day when we see each other. In any case, I had to
leave. Berlin wasn't far enough – I wanted to leave the
country. I was lucky. Shortly after I arrived here in
New York, I found a job in an architect's office, and
after becoming an American citizen, I started working in
the New York City Department of Buildings. I became
Deputy Commissioner there, which sounds a lot grander
than it is. Mainly, I looked at development plans and
issued permits. Unfortunately, I had some ideas that
my superiors did not like, and at some point, my work
was no longer compatible with my involvement in
neighbourhood politics.

After being laid off, I locked myself in my
apartment for weeks and worried about how I was
going to earn a living. But in the end, being fired was
a blessing in disguise. At the moment, I'm keeping
afloat with publications in small architectural
newspapers, have learned a lot and am now even
writing a book.

If I'm not at home working, I often sit in Washington
Square Park, where I'm also writing this letter to you. I
like to sit here on the steps in front of the fountain and
watch the people. They play folk music, much to the
annoyance of the police and the residents, who get upset
about the 'beatniks'. I realise that I'm an old woman
in the eyes of these students, but I like to hang out with
young people. They remind me of how we used to be and
how other people saw our freedom as a provocation.
Such people will probably always exist – even if
everything that we have fought to liberate has now been
put back in its box. The fear of extremes is now greater
than the fear of boredom.

When I get up from my step, I can barely see the
top of the new PanAm building in Midtown. They're
building like crazy, and it's supposed to open next year.
It is Gropius' first skyscraper and will be the highest
office building in the city. It is exactly what people now
consider modern: taller, bigger, more phallic.

Recently, I was invited to a dinner party in one
of the elegant apartments on the Upper East Side.
Charlotte, an old friend of mine, whom you may
have met in Berlin, dragged me there. I followed her
past the porter to the thirteenth floor, and suddenly
I was in a Bauhaus museum: Breuer's chairs were
everywhere, and on the walls hung paintings by
Kandinsky and Klee. It was the strangest journey
through time! Tell me, how do you feel now about the
ideas we had back then? Oh, there's probably no need
to ask – you already knew what you wanted. Your

carpets are still a great success, if I understood your letter right. A school of your own, Maria, how happy I am for you!

Let's hope we can see each other again in Israel or Europe, if I can raise money for the trip. And of course you're always very welcome here in New York. I would love to sit on my bed with you again and talk for hours.

Big hugs and send your family warm greetings from me!

Luise

18.05.1959

Today was a good day – one of those mild spring days in New York that I love so much. Where the sun lingers until dinner, you can push open the window and listen to the neighbours talking across the fire escapes.

I walked all the way from the office through the city and thought about what a strange situation I've landed in yet again. Why was I of all people chosen to check the plans of the PanAm building? The New York City Department of Buildings has 1,200 employees, damn it! And so, I meet Gropius again. Or, rather, his ideas. My first instinct was a base one. Well, if I have the opportunity to sabotage Gropius' first project in New York, why shouldn't I take it? Especially since his building is certainly not going to be a beauty.

When I got home, though, I thought of something better. I'll dish out permits by the dozen, fill them in with the most beautiful handwriting, and he'll never know who is behind it. Let him build his soulless office block if he wants to. I'll happily watch him from afar.

Now I sit here at my desk, looking out at the street where the children across the street are playing double Dutch, inhaling the warm air and feeling extremely pleased with myself.

Bank of America – Safe Deposit Box Inventory

This inventory is available for your convenience in keeping an accurate record of the contents of your safe deposit box. Keep an inventory list in your box and a copy at your home or office.

Date Deposited	Description of Item
03.02.1960	Gold necklace with pendant, gemstone ruby
03.02.1960	Banknote dated 1923, 'Two Hundred Billion Marks'
03.02.1960	Ashtray, workshop Marianne Brandt, brass and stainless steel
03.02.1960	Lease for 208 West 10th Street
03.02.1960	Book, Bruno Taut, *The Dissolution of Cities*
03.02.1960	Ticket, Carnegie Hall, 1943
03.02.1960	Cufflinks, silver, green stone
03.02.1960	Housing estate plans (blueprint), seven pages
03.02.1960	Wall hanging, woven, multi-color

Bringing a book from manuscript to what you are reading is a team effort.

Dialogue Books would like to thank everyone at Little, Brown who helped to publish *Blueprint* in the UK.

Editorial
Sharmaine Lovegrove
Sophia Schoepfer
Thalia Proctor

Contracts
Melanie Leggett

Sales
Andrew Cattanach
Viki Cheung
Ben Goddard
Rachael Hum
Hannah Methuen

Publicity
Kimberley Nyanhondera

Marketing
Emily Moran
Hermione Ireland
Hillary Tisman

Design
Helen Bergh
Nick Evans

Production
Narges Nojoumi
Nick Ross
Mike Young

Copy Editor
Alison Tulett

Proof Reader
Loma Halden